200 MONOLOGUES

One-Minute Monologues for Teens and Adults

Michael McClendon

ISBN: 979-8-3552-0867-7

The words are only the vehicle. You, my talented friend, are the driver.

Exact Change

I didn't come in to complain, only explain. See, I'm vegetarian. So I know I didn't order the double-decker moo-cow bacon-porker Spam burger bowel-blaster with extra grease and a chili cheesedog on the side. And even if I did order the hotdogger artery clogger, it would be awful hard to choke that down without something to drink, and the closest thing in this bag to a soda is this package of Hickory Heat hot sauce and forty packets of salt. So I stand by the fact that you gave me the wrong order. And I'm just as certain you gave me the wrong change. But since you shouted at me through the Happy Hog's mouth that you *do not make mistakes*, I have to take you at your word. I just had to come inside before I drove off to let you know that the change you gave me was not in *your* favor, but in *mine*. So thanks for the extra fifty bucks and have a Happy Hog of a day. See ya!

Car Talk

Different car keys can sometimes fit into different cars of the same *make*. How was I to know? I'm not even sure what *make* I drive! I just know it goes *varoom*, drinks gas, and is a pretty blue when I have time to wash it. And yes, I did see you run through the parking lot screaming at me, but it's not as if that hasn't happened to me before. Usually, it just means I got the last on-sale frozen turkey at Best Buy, and some irate housewife is trying to snatch it from me. How was I to know I was driving away in your car? Your taste in music appears to be the same as mine. And you have just as much bird poo on the windshield as I do. And you even have the same bobblehead on the dashboard, so give me a break! Now if you'll just get in, I'll drive you back to my car and we'll switch. No, you'll have to get in the back. Your husband's still asleep in the front.

Cheerleader

I thought she was the most beautiful girl I'd ever seen. But she was a senior, one year ahead of me, so that put her out of my league. And she was a cheerleader, so that put her even further from my reach. I had a lit class with her, but I sat in front, so I never got to look at her there. I used to watch her in the hall: books pressed to her bosom and blond hair swinging back and forth with every step she took. Everyone seemed to know her, and she smiled at them all. Oh, that smile! I always thought that if she would smile—just smile at me—I would be transformed. But that could never be. I was a nerd. And she was a cheerleader.

Re-tread

My aunt bought a fake butt. What happened to her old butt? I mean, did it just wear out? When I was little and I did something bad, my mom would say, "I'm gonna wear your butt *out*!" Is that what happened? Did she do something really awful, and her mom spanked her until her butt wore out?

Or did she lose it? I once heard of a man who lost his butt in the stock market. Maybe she should go to the market and look for it.

Or maybe she just needed a new one. I once heard her say she was so tired, her butt was dragging.

Well, if she lost her butt, she should get a new one. But if it's only dragging or wore out, why doesn't she just get a re-tread?

Ironing Day

How are you feeling? They just took me in to see the baby. I am so proud of you! We have a little son, a little boy! Yes, they tell me he is perfectly happy and healthy. Yes, he has all his fingers and toes. I counted them every one, just like you asked me to. And guess what? He has a full head of hair, and it's a beautiful brown, just like yours!   But can I ask you just one thing about him? And I'm not being critical or anything. But I know he's all cleaned up and, well, finished, and this is how we'll be taking him home. So. How do we get the wrinkles out?

Spelcheck

Yes, ma'am. That is my esay. Well, you asked us to write an esay on "How to Make the World a Better Place." So I wrote, "Don't make us write any more dumb esays." Yes, that's it, the whole thing. No, ma'am, I didn't think you would find that entirely too short. I like to think of it as economical. No, ma'am, I didn't know *esay* was spelled with two *s*'s. Well, how am I supposed to look up how to spell *esay* if I don't know how to spell it?

Yes, ma'am, I do think an hour will be long enough for me to learn how to spell *detention*.

Determined

You can say whatever you want about me. Go ahead. Won't bother me one bit.

Except for one thing: never say I didn't try. I try. I get up. *I show up, and I do my best!* I go on when I can't go on, and I keep trying even when I don't know what it is I'm trying. This is where I will take exception. You will not criticize me for lack of trying. So cut loose. Tear me down. Make a list of my faults and put them on the six o'clock news. But you can't say I didn't try.

(Almost as an afterthought) Hey, I just thought of what I want on my headstone: *She (He) showed up.*

Niblets

Why do I get detention?

I was sitting in the lunchroom, minding my own business, when I got hit with pudding. Pudding! And when I turned around, the girls who threw it hit me with mashed potatoes! So I picked up a handful of corn niblets and heaved it right at her. After pudding and potatoes, I'd say I had a right to defend myself with any food group available. Unfortunately, that's when Ms. Brooks walked into the cafeteria and my niblets hit her instead. She freaked. I ran right up to her and said, "What's wrong, what's wrong?" and she said, "I've got corn in my bra, and I've never had anything in my bra before." Well, that last part struck me as funny, and I'll admit I laughed.

Principal Carol, I just hope that someday you know the pain of having pudding in your hair and niblets in your bra.

Fuzzy Thoughts

Dogs are really people. Little people in fuzzy suits. And maybe they're even smarter than we are. I mean, they sleep whenever and wherever they want to. We bring them food and water and love, brush them and carry them and clean up their poopy. They can entertain themselves for hours with a bone or rubber toy.

Sometimes, I look into those soft brown eyes and realize they are probably thinking, *Humans are really dogs. Big dogs without fur. Maybe that's why they have to wear clothes.*

Rainy Day

      Grandma, can I wear your good wig? Why not? You're not using it; it's not Sunday. Then can I ride in your chair? C'mon, what's the use of having a Hoveround if you can't lay a little rubber from time to time? Okay then, can I wear your hearing aid? How about your glasses? Can I use your bifocals to make everything look all fuzzy? Then can I play with your teeth? Let me chase the dog around with your dentures.

      You never let me have any fun. When I get old, I am not going to be so selfish with my spare parts.

Purr

Out of all the doors and all the houses and all the streets, you stopped at ours. What made you choose us? And you meowed and meowed until we opened the door. And you came inside, just like you knew what you were doing. I remember how you ran between my feet and went right to the kitchen and just stared and waited. How did you know to do that? That was a long time ago, wasn't it? I bet you don't even remember. We didn't know you then. We didn't even know you were ours. But you knew.

Self-Serve

Thank you, honey, for pumping the gas. See, it's much quicker when I go inside and pay and you pump the gas! And now we're back on the road again with coffee and donuts and—what is that bumping noise? Listen. I'm sure I hear a rhythmic bumping. No, it doesn't sound like the engine. It sounds like something outside the car.

Uh, did you put the hose back after you pumped the gas?

Don't cry, honey. We can mail it back to them.

Pass It Around

Well, I appreciate that. But I don't think of helping out here at the shelter as doing anyone a favor. It's more like you doing me a favor. See, when I walk out of here, I feel lighter, as if I've left some burden behind. I feel more worthy, like I've earned a little bit more of the happiness that is showered upon me like gentle rain from the heavens. And though I may be draggin' low when I come in, your smile pumps me up so much that sometimes I just go home and clean something that doesn't need cleaning. So don't ever think that you are less than me. Never feel like you're the taker and I'm the giver. No, we all just pass it around, don't we? So thank you for allowing me to pass something on to you. See, someone did that same thing for me once; once upon a time, when I was sitting right where you are now.

Frantic

I can't clean under my bed! It's not that I'm lazy, and I'm not a slob. It's a matter of life and death! I saw this movie once where a kid looked under his bed and a demon clown was hiding under it and grabbed him and pulled him to a horrible bloody death. Now, do you want that on your head? Do you really think you can stand the guilt? Is the life of your only child worth nothing more than a few dust bunnies and some lost underwear? I ask you sincerely. Can you really send me off to my doom?

Well, it was worth a try.

Always

I had a brother. But he died before I was born. But I still think about him. I always wonder what it would be like if he had lived; what would it feel like to have a big brother? Would he be nice to me? Would he protect me? What kinds of things would we do, talk about? I think about him a lot. He's, in some ways, very much alive to me. And when somebody asks if I have any brothers or sisters, I say yes. Yes, I did.

Daddy Complex

I can't get used to being called Daddy. That's a name for other guys, guys with grey hair and condos and retirement plans and plaid pants. Dads have riding lawnmowers. Dads have answers. Dads make decisions. Dads have yellow toenails. Dads are smart and calm and wise, and they sit in recliners and fall asleep with the newspaper over their face. Hey, I don't even loosen my belt after dinner! I never talk about the good ole days, and I have never ever even once said, "Kids these days!" Oh, and I don't know how to putter. I can't be a daddy. I'm too young. I don't know how.

Grinding Fear

Could you please just put me to sleep? I don't trust painkillers, and you may say you're going to numb the area, but how can I be sure? And even if I can't feel it, I can see. And if I see you coming toward me with those *instruments,* I'm going to flinch, I just know it. And listen, what if I *hear stuff.* Even if I close my eyes tight, I'll hear whirring and sloshing, and this will make me crazy, I tell ya, plain crazy. So please just knock me out. Put me under. Make sure there are no brain waves before you even think about doing this to me. Help me, I'm beggin' ya! I can't take it, I tell ya, I can't take it!

I *really* hate having my teeth cleaned.

Final

      I waited until the others were gone. I wanted to wait until it was quiet and empty before I said my good-bye. Because you have been my best friend, and I never told you that. That's the one thing I would change if I could. I'd let you know that you are my best friend. I don't think I deserve someone like you in my life, yet there you were at every turn and corner. There you were. And I couldn't let you go without saying it.

Home Sweet Home

I wish I could live in Home Depot. I'd wake up every morning and mow something in the Garden Center, then kill something with pesticides. I'd rewire everything in sight, caulk anything that leaks, ride over to Lumber in a John Deere, and cut something, plane it, sand it, paint it, seal it, then feed it all into a wood chipper and mulch to my heart's content. Yeah, it's only a dream, but it's a good dream: unlimited power tools and thirty-seven styles of toilets. What else could a man want?

Educational Vacation

This year, my family saw the Grand Canyon, which was basically a huge ditch that used to have some water in the bottom. And we saw the Mississippi River, which I thought would have worked much better in the Grand Canyon, then they wouldn't have to build all those bridges over the river, plus the canyon wouldn't be so far if you fell in, which I almost did. We also got to see the world's biggest ball of chewing gum, which made me totally gag because I started thinking it was probably mostly spit, and also, who put it all together, and did they wash their hands after? And then, we saw Mount Rushmore, which was actually very cool. Way up high on a mountain, there were these huge heads of dead guys carved out of stone. Now, this makes you think: how many years did it take the wind to wear away all that rock just in the perfect shape of those dead guys?

Country Store

I remember one afternoon, as I studied the boxes of candy and racks of pork rinds and potato chips, an old man stood looking out the storefront window. The sky had begun to rain, and I expected him to wait with the rest of us. But no, he pushed open the cranky screen and walked right out into the downpour. I followed and pressed my face against the mesh, watching to see which car he'd get into. Strangers were rare and brought out natural curiosity to those of us who lived here. He walked beyond the one car, then the Ford truck, and finally past the flatbed wagon. He turned left and headed slowly away from town, his hands in his pockets, his face straight ahead. I watched him till he was lost in the grey wetness. I couldn't imagine where he was going or how he got here in the first place. I wondered who could have left him and why they were not here to pick him up. I wanted to ask him why he didn't wait until the rain stopped and why he walked so casually, as if the rain didn't matter to him at all.

Surveillance

They're watching me. No, I'm not paranoid. They're really watching me. And listening. How else can they tell how many pay-per-view movies I see?   And how about my cell phone? When I change time zones, *the time changes on my phone!* And what about my GPS? They know where I am and how fast I got there! They know if I stop to eat and where I stopped to eat—do they know *what* I ate? But worst of all are the public restrooms. I reach for the faucet, and the waters turns on. I reach for the dryer, and the hot air begins to blow. Every time something flushes, I just think, *How did they know I was finished?*

Go Figure

I am so happy for you! Yes, I am just beside myself with happiness that you can still fit into your high school prom dress. How delightful that you haven't gained *one single ounce* in all this time! But tell me, do many of your current social occasions call for a Velveeta orange gown with a hoop skirt and lime green roses on the shoulder? And do you attend many events nowadays that call for you to wear your homecoming tiara and sash? Well, you're not the only one who can still fit into her prom dress. I can still wear mine.

As a sock.

Trade-Off

Is it really worth it? Is gossip so much fun that you just cannot stop yourself? Do you find it entertaining? Fulfilling? Does it complete you? I wonder if you would say the same thing *to* a person that you say *about* them. And how do you think you would feel if you were the target of gossip instead of the one doing the talking? Well, I wish you the best. I sincerely hope that you enjoy the time you spend tearing people down and gossiping with your little group. Because it just cost you a friend.

Switch Hitter

Do you have a very unhappy little boy in your ballet class? He'd be about so high, has a scab on his nose, and would probably be very, very bad at twirling and leaping. Because I just tried to leave a little girl in a tutu at football practice. Hey, don't judge me! You try playing taxi to fourteen brats on a sugar high and see if you don't get a little bit confused! Okay, so I suppose I could have been a little more observant. In hindsight, I suppose the kicking and screaming should have given me a clue when I was dropping him off at *Miss Trudy's Tour je Tots*. That, and the helmet.

Amateur

I was a contestant in an amateur contest once. It was one of the happiest days of my life, the first time I felt really accepted. No, I didn't win. In fact, I didn't even place. I hardly even got applause for my performance. And at the time, I had no idea what *amateur* even meant. But after the contest, I stood, totally satisfied, complete, overjoyed. Because the one of the judges walked up to me afterward. He looked me straight in the eye, and he said, *"Kid, you certainly are an amateur."*

Technically Challenged

Don't you hate it when your parents tell you about how great things were back in their day? I don't see how things could have been so cool back in the day. In fact, I don't think I really believe most of the things they tell me. Watching movies outside in a parking lot? Really? And televisions that only got three channels. Come on! And in the olden days, they didn't have cell phones. At least that's what my parents tell me every time I go over my monthly minutes. No cell phones? Seriously? They expect me to believe that! What did they do, carry their laptops with them all the time?

Re-Action Figures

Dolls are cool. Doesn't matter if you are a boy or a girl, dolls are cool. Just pop the head off one and put it on another and you have a whole new creature. Or put a dinosaur tail on a Betsy Wetsy. Or attach toy truck tires to their feet. Baby dolls with animal heads are great for scaring little kids. Baby dolls without any heads are great for scaring big kids. But best of all are the GI Joes and Barbies. Just switch their clothes and watch your parents start looking for a therapist.

Pet Delivery

Dog treats are being mysteriously delivered to our house. The FedEx man keeps showing up with boxes of rawhide chews, fuzzy toys, snuggly beds, and bacon-flavored treats. Each day brings a new delivery of pork ears, cat-shaped chew toys, and peanut butter bites. Oh, Thumper is a happy, happy dog these days, but nobody will admit ordering doggie treats online. It was all a big mystery until we finally found evidence that cannot be denied: drool on the laptop and paw prints on the keys.

Nursing Home

When I was little, my parents took me to a nursing home. Now, I had a little brother and two baby sisters, so I knew what nursing meant. I could hardly contain myself as we pulled up to the nursing home. I was looking forward to playing with all the babies, feeding them from bottles, and rocking them to sleep. Open the doors, and let me see all those sweet little bundles in pink and blue!

Boy, was I surprised.

Home Ec

I love my mom, but she's the worst cook in the world. No, seriously. The worst cook in the world. Her food damages the silverware. Raccoons won't eat out of our trash anymore. I suppose it would help if she wouldn't try to be so creative. We never know what to expect. Is it a dessert? Is it an entrée? Is it floor wax? I tried to eat the centerpiece once. Actually, it was something of an improvement over her pork ice cream with lima bean sauce.

Mine

You sit there looking all sleek and aloof. But you know I'm watching you. And you think I want you, don't you? Yeah, you're right about that. I want you. Bad. And you think you're in control, don't you? But I know something that you don't. I know you're coming home with me. And you got nothing to say about it. And every guy in the neighborhood will stare when I take you out. And they'll all want you, but you're mine, all mine. And you got nothing to say about it. Give it up because soon, I'm gonna own you, baby. You just let me get out my checkbook. Harley Davidson, you're mine.

At Capacity

I don't know how I feel about these Huggies. I mean, sure, it's a pain washing dirty cloth diapers, but somehow this seems so unsanitary! Maybe it's just me. After all, if the other parents are using them, who am I to disagree? And the company that makes them, they must know what they're doing.   So I'll just follow the directions and leave them on until they fill to their capacity. And this size says—wow—up to nine pounds!

Retro

Honey, could you come in here a minute? Well, I was trying on my parachute pants from college. Man, I still got it! But there's something wrong with them. I think you must have shrunk them in the dryer. They still look the same, but they get stuck when I try to zip them up! Wow, who knew they'd draw up so much over the years? Maybe if I put a little slit in the back and then tie a sweater around it...

Honey, when you bring the scissors, could you bring my arch supports and corn pads? I just found my disco platforms!

OCD OCD OCD

I do not have OCD. I do not have OCD. I do not have OCD. I just have to check and make sure the door is locked, and eighteen is a good safe number of times to lock and unlock it. And it's an established fact that if you stack your canned goods by fiber content, they just look better and the earth will be safe from asteroids. And if you don't touch your nose ten times before each bite, the oceans will dry up. And paper money should always be facing the same direction and in order of descending value because it just fits in your wallet better. And it keeps vampires away. When was the last time you saw a vampire in our neighborhood? See, it works.

Don't judge me. I am not OCD. I am thorough.

Web Master

Okay, I saw *Charlotte's Web* and found it to be absolutely delightful. But you don't look like the type of spider who sings and tells stories and sounds like Julia Roberts. No, you look like a spider who would crawl over my face at night or hide in a shoe just waiting to bite me or lay eggs in my ear and let your children feed on my brain. So I apologize in advance if this is considered animal abuse. I'm really a very gentle person. But you are hairy and scary, and we are not compatible roommates. So just sit there dreaming of gnawing off my arm, and I'll introduce you to my little friend: Mr. Magazine!

Mirror Image

What do you mean you don't have this in my size? I'm a size 4, and this entire rack is filled with size 4! I would certainly know my own size better than you, wouldn't I? Okay, I'll admit you are laboring under a false impression. It's these mirrors. You have fat mirrors. This store has fat mirrors, and they do make me look like a "before" picture from a Lipozene ad. But it's just an optical illusion created by your fat mirrors. Now please bring that dress, in a size 4, into the dressing room.

Just in case they run a little small, bring it in a size 8 too.

Pavlov with a P

What do you mean I can't get my money back for the dog training sessions? You were supposed to housebreak him, not teach him to break the house. Okay, to be fair, you did teach him to "go" on command, but now he can't tell the difference between a command and a conversation. Every time he hears the—uh, (*whispered*) the sixteenth letter of the alphabet—he leaves us a little puddle. We're all going to have to learn sign language. There's one particular vegetable we can't even serve for dinner anymore. Can you just dumb him down a little?

Graceful Aging

My grandpa is so cool. He sees people that nobody else sees. And he wears his clothes in a really unique way, like backwards and inside out. And sometimes, he wears his undies over his pants. Grandpa tells me really neat stories about things he used to do, although I think some of them were just things he saw on shows like *Barnaby Jones* and *The Love Boat*. But it's okay with me if he thinks he was once married to Angie Dickinson. I don't really know who that is either. I think she was a Charlie's Angel or a Flying Nun.

ID

I'm sorry already, but it's not my fault! Next time, I'll look a little closer. Can I help it if all little kids look alike? Can I help it if they all wear the same dirty little clothes? Yeah, he was kicking and screaming, but that's not unusual, they all do that too! Hey, next time you want me to go out and bring my little brother home, you might want to make it a little easier for me. How about a name tag or—microchips are nice.

Single Life

I am not going out on dates. Never ever. What's fun about dating? You have to get cleaned up. And I mean everything, even your ears. And you have to wear clean clothes with socks and a belt. You can't scratch or yawn or wipe your nose on anything but a handkerchief. Seriously, a handkerchief when I've got two perfectly good sleeves? And you have to smile and say stupid things like "I had *such* a good time"—even if you didn't! And you have to open doors and pay for everything, and sometimes, you even have to *kiss her!* But worst of all, dating can lead to terrible things. And hey, I'm too young to get married!

Fiber Content

I have the best parents in the world. They tell me everything I do is the best, and they never criticize when I make mistakes. Like I made dinner for them last night. Okay, it was just frozen pizza, but they "oohed" and "aaahed" and smiled and ate every bite. Afterwards, they told me how sweet I was to fix the food and how much they enjoyed it. Never once did they mention it was tough or too chewy. But next time, I'll know: remove cardboard before serving.

The Perfect Gift

Baby, are you sure you need me with you? I don't really care what we get them for their wedding. You go. You register for the gifts. Why do you even need me?   They'll never know I didn't stand in line, as long as you sign my name. Here, take the credit card and have a blast. Get 'em a gravy boat or some barbecue tongs or maybe some of those little toilet soaps that look like shells that nobody can use. Yeah, you just go look at all the pretty little dishes and towels and things and paste stickers on the ones you want.

What? A gun? You get to use a gun? Let's go register!

Permanent Solution

Grandpa, you know you're my favorite grandpa, right? And I can talk to you about anything, right? Well, I was wondering about your false teeth. I know you take them out at night and put them back in every day. But sometimes when you are talking, they clack and start to come out all by themselves, don't they? And you don't like that, do you? Um, you know that sticky stuff that you put under your dentures? Yeah, the goo that holds them in place. Well, have you ever noticed how much that tube looks like the tube of *Superglue?* No, I'm not saying the tubes got mixed up, but well...how would you feel about having permanent teeth again?

Best Seat in the House

Oh, no, please don't sit there. I'm saving this seat for someone; could you please not sit there? For real, this seat needs to stay vacant. *Hey*! You really need to listen to me. This seat isn't for you. I'm claiming it, and I'm holding it. Now I'm asking you one last time. Please do not take this seat!

Seriously, this is a fact and not a threat. You are going to be sorry if you take this seat, and that's a promise.

And you're sitting anyway. See? I was just trying to be a nice person.

Yep, someone threw up in it.

For those who Think Young

When did I get old? When did I drop out of the in crowd? When did I start using phrases like "in crowd"? At what point did I decide most people drive too fast and most rooms are too cold? And what was the exact date when I first fell asleep in front of the TV? How long have I been noticing hair in my brush and in the drain? When did technology begin to scare me? Oh, I can send e-mails, and most of the time, I can get my smartphone to work. But try as I may, I can't get a grip on the FaceTwitter or that WebBrowse thingy, and I can't Skypemaster like all the kids today. I just said, "Kids today." I have officially become my dad.

Dream Date

Excuse me, but could you please stop smacking your gum so loudly? Because it's distracting and irritating, and there's a rule against chewing gum in here. Seriously, you can give me that "I'm too cool for the rule" look all you want, but rules apply to pretty, empty-headed people just like the rest of us. If you want to be really appealing, you might consider how you look when you chomp and drool and smack on gum while trying to make a date. Oh, it's not gum? It's tobacco. My, you are a real catch, aren't you?

And by the way. You have a booger.

Toxic

What is that smell? I thought it was the fridge, but now it's near the hamper. Come over here and see if you smell it. Smell it now? Wow, that's terrible! And it's everywhere. It's over by the sink now, and—come over here—now it's by the table. Try the cabinets. Yep, it's over here too. It's like it's an entity, like it's moving. It's everywhere. It's everywhere...that you are. Dude! That should be illegal. How can you live with yourself? I think I've figured out what's causing the hole in the ozone.

Perfect Figure

I am so tired of commercials that tell me what I should look like. After nine hours of work, picking up the kids, doing the shopping, making dinner, and cleaning up the house, please forgive me if I don't feel like dancing around the house in lace undies. And heaven help me if my hair is showing a touch of gray or doesn't cascade about my shoulders like an auburn waterfall. And please, please, can they just have one woman on TV who actually has hips and thighs? If I was willing to have three almonds and a Tic Tac for dinner, I could look like that too. Well, almost. I'd still need implants, hair extensions, lip injections, and legs up to my chin. Oh, and attitude. Don't forget the 'tude.

Family Skeletons

Did you ever see that movie *The Exorcist?* And that little girl threw up green pea soup and her head spun around and they had to tie her to the bed? And she was so horrible that even her mother didn't want to go into the room? And she had terrible breath and used foul language and killed people and threw furniture? Yeah, well, that pretty much describes my sisters. Just wanted to warn you before we go inside.

Hero

I found a photo of my dad. He was standing beside a red convertible and was wearing a white sport coat and holding some flowers in his left hand. A pink carnation was pinned to his lapel, and his hair—well, he had hair! And lots of it, and it was swirled back in a ducktail. I think he must have been headed to pick up a girl for the prom or maybe a Saturday night dance. Maybe my mom. Who knows? Looking at that creased picture, looking at that boy standing on the sidewalk on a late spring afternoon, I saw my dad as person for the first time. He's not a superhero, but he tries to be one for me. He was just a guy. Like me. I think I need to give him a hug.

Mommy

He called me mommy. I didn't know what to do. Of course, I'd heard of this before, but it had never happened to me. I just stood there. I knew what was going to happen next, and of course, it did. Starting like a wave, the laughter ran all around the room. His face got red and then redder and then I felt my face get red, but still I just stood there. Hey, it's not that unusual for a student to slip and call their teacher Mom or Mommy. Mom would have been bad enough. But he said Mommy. And then of course, he is eighteen.

Olympic Surfing

Used to be just one sports channel. And that was only active on weekends. Then there were three. Now there are twenty-four–hour channels for hockey, bowling, football, basketball, surfing, snowboarding, soccer, tennis, polo, skiing, baseball, pinball, fishing, camping, hiking, bicycle racing, car racing, horse racing, dog racing, pinball, and jousting. Navigating between all these different sports channels takes real skill. Hey, maybe channel surfing the sports channels should become a sport. I'd watch.

Picky Picky

I ran into my old homeroom teacher the other day. Well, "ran into" is not exactly the right phrase. I was in the fresh fruits section at the Better Buy and saw this really familiar-looking woman thumping cantaloupes. Man, something about the way she laid into those poor melons gave me chills. Those talons could have cracked coconuts. Then I spotted the stern gray hair tortured back into a lifeless bun and those cat-eye glasses with the long chain, and all my middle-school fears returned. And then, right before my eyes, she started picking her nose! This is the woman who gave me demerits for chewing gum! Shame on you, Ms. Thorndike! And right in front of the melons too.

Tele-Logic

So I was watching this movie from back in the olden days—like back in the nineties!—and this guy is walking down the street, see? And he stops at this little building and goes inside. Now the building is just about big enough to fit one person in it, and it's made completely out of glass. So he goes inside and shuts the glass door. And he lifts up this thing on a cord that's attached to a big black box. And he puts money into the black box. And then he starts to talk into it—yeah, it's a telephone! I couldn't believe it! I mean, why didn't he just use his cell?

Showdown in Aisle 9

Lady, you took my shopping cart. You just walked right up and started off with it.

This happens every time I come to Wal-Mart. I watch people walk in the door without a cart, and then, suddenly, they have a cart. Why don't you just get one when you walk in? Oh, wait, I know the answer to that one—you were only going to pick up two items, but then you saw something on sale and then you remembered you needed milk and...

No, I'm not giving in this time. It's my cart.

How about this: without looking down, name the items in the cart. Can't do it, can you? Well, I can. There's one pair of work boots, four cans of Spam, a box of kitty litter, frozen peas, some Midol, and a box of Jimmy Dean's Breakfast Biscuits.

Ah, victory in the frozen foods aisle. What a rush!

Disconnect

(Hastily grabbing phone.) Hey, honey, thanks so much for calling back! Don't talk—just listen. I only have a few seconds here. First: Frankie still has diarrhea. *Please* stop on your way home and pick up his prescription. There's poop all over the house, and everything I put in one end just shoots out the other. Next, I'm going to leave your mother to you—if she doesn't start closing her robe or at least start wearing something under it, I'm going to duct-tape her clothes to her sagging body. Judy's parakeet died. If we can find one that looks similar, I don't think she'll ever know I flushed the other one. Now, I picked up the Preparation H you asked for, so you don't have any excuse for skipping church except for being bored.

Oh.

Hello, Reverend Hartley.

Kiss Off

Why won't I let you take me out?   Think really hard, Brandon.

It might be because you made the entire lunchroom want to puke when you drank chocolate milk through your nose. What about the time I let you drive me home from church, and you steered the entire time with your knees?   And those piercings are not cool, they're just nasty. Hey, how about the fact that you wear your pants so low that we can see your underwear? Not to mention the fact that last Thursday, you forgot to *wear* underwear. Oh, and if you think that makes you look *(using fingers for air quotes)* "street," I don't think anyone can qualify as *(air quotes again)* "street" while they live at home and get lunch money from their mommy.

So hitch up your pants and buy a clue, Brandon. I babysit on weekends. Not on dates.

Straight Flush

Automatic restrooms scare me.

I can't help it. Every time I visit one, I come out feeling that I've been violated.

I step away from a urinal, and it knows it. It *knows*. I just find that disturbing. How much does it know? And exactly what does it see? If I walk up to a urinal but don't do anything, would it still flush? I'm not sure I want to know.

And automatic faucets: if they can turn on the water because they know I need to wash my hands, do they know if I *don't* wash my hands?

And of course, there's the scariest of all: the automatic toilet. This brings up issues that I don't even want to discuss.

Sometimes, when I leave a public restroom, I feel like I should say thanks.

But I don't.

I'm afraid I might get an answer.

Truth in Advertising

I think you should be honest with him. Now. Before the wedding.

Well, you know those diet meals in the frozen food aisle? You get them home and you take them out of the box, and you find padding and plastic and boxes within cartons, and by the time you get it all open, you know why it's diet—there are three molecules of food. I'm afraid that's what you're selling your fiancé—all package. Remember, I know about the false eyelashes and the hair dye and the corset and the padding. I was there when you had your eyebrows tattooed on and the hair weaves done. I helped you buy the pushup bra and everything that it pushes up.

You're a great girl. And I know he loves you. But tell him everything now. If he's getting a Slim-fast, don't advertise a Happy Meal.

Jobsite Clarity

What do you mean when you say we are having a *mandatory voluntary workday?*

Now, I can understand having a voluntary workday. And I understand the word *mandatory.* It's just that this phrase was picking at my brain all night: *mandatory voluntary.* That phrase makes no sense; those two words do not fit together. It's like saying military *intelligence* or jumbo *shrimp* or rap *music.*

So please indulge my obsessive-compulsive nature and make me understand what *mandatory voluntary workday* means.

(Pause.)

Yes, I do understand the phrase *terminated without benefits.*

Thank you for clearing that up.

Family History

You want to know why we never have sleepovers at my house?

Shame.

Humiliation.

My family.

My grandfather likes to hunt by hanging his rifle out the window of his truck while driving seventy-five miles an hour. When my grandmother remembers to wear anything at all under her robe, it's usually high heels and a tube top. One of my little brothers likes to play in the litter box, so the cats tend to use the kitchen sink. Another brother wears a *Friday the 13th* hockey mask 24/7, and another one only speaks by clicking and popping like an Aborigine. We have a 300-pound pig named Daisy who sleeps...well, anywhere she wants to—she's a 300-pound pig. My dad's a survivalist and my mom's a Democrat.

The horror.

Oh, the horror.

Choreography

People love to watch me dance.

Oh, I'm not any good. In fact, I'm a nightmare on the dance floor. I've been called spastic and scary and a lot of other things. Someone once said I looked like I was fighting off a swarm of angry bees. Then someone else said that bees wouldn't come near me if I was dancing like that.

But I dance because I like to. I love the feeling of using every part of my body to react to the music. I can't help it if the different parts of my body don't communicate with each other. I do a lot of damage on the dance floor, but I always have lots of room. And there are other benefits as well. Once, I started dancing on the sidewalk while waiting for a light to change. My hat fell off while I was getting down with my own bad self. When I picked it up, I found a chiropractor's business card and three dollars and forty-five cents in change.

Second Chance

I'm thinking about getting married. I know who I want to marry. But it's hard for me to ask her.

See, I've been hurt before. She was beautiful and smart and could swing by her legs on the monkey bars. She had freckles and a scab on her nose, and she punched me on the playground. She was the love of my life.

I was sure she would marry me. But when I asked her she just said, "Yuck!" and walked off toward the swings.

But I have lived to love another day. Yes, I'm thinking about getting married.

New Arrival

(Fast and furious) All right, now hear this: You may have the cuteness factor going for you, but I have age and experience on my side. Yes, you're all new and you're the precious little baby, but if you think you can take my place, you are wrong, wrong, wrong. I've been the baby in this family ever since I was born, and I am not giving it up to some little wah-wah-wah, crybaby, vomit-monkey, poop-factory. And hey, you're just my niece; I don't think you're even really a member of my family, and there's no law that says I have to put up with you. So just stay out of my way and—

(Immediately going through a complete change) Mom! Mom, come in here! My precious little niece just smiled at me! Yes, she did! Yes, my widdle angel did! Widdy biddy precious baby!

Home Improvement

(Speaking in a loud voice to husband outside the house)
Baby, are you sure you should try to cut down that tree? I mean, it's already leaning right over the house.

Oh, honey, of course I believe in you. But let's not forget the toilet you tried to replace. *(Under her breath)* And I am so over having to use the Texaco station. *(Loud again)* Or the gas stove you tried to install. *(To herself)* I don't think my eyebrows are *ever* gonna grow back.

Sugar? *Baby?* If you keep cutting at that angle, isn't it going to fall *toward* the house?

I am not believing you are sitting *on* the limb that you are cutting off. Don't you know that when it falls—*(Eyes growing wide)* Kids, grab the dog, you're daddy's comin' in for a landing!

Family Tradition

We had to bring my great-grandpa with us because he can't be left in the house alone. Great-grandpa sometimes thinks the closet is the bathroom.

He gets confused and told some people that we put him in the *veterinarian's* hospital for his operation. But then, this is the man who once stood in a hotel maid's pantry for twenty minutes, waiting for it to take him to the seventeenth floor.

Once, in an airplane, his ears stopped up, and he started freaking out, trying to get them to open up. The stewardess was yelling at him, "Drop your jaws, drop your *jaws!*" *(Pause)* But he misunderstood.

I think being old is really cool. I can't wait till I can get away with mooning a stewardess and peeing in the closet.

Tune-Up

C'mere, young man. Let's look under my car hood together. First of all, that thing you called a doohickey is the air filter, and it's just fine; I'd say good for at least another thousand miles. The pink color of my transmission fluid is normal and indicates that it does *not* need to be changed, and if you'll replace that battery cable you just loosened, I'm sure my car will start just fine.

Now, replacing the valve cover gasket should take under thirty minutes and cost a hundred-fourteen dollars plus tax. If you don't want to do it, I can always take it over to Precision Tune, *after* I stop by the Better Business Bureau and the sheriff's office.

Don't mess with Mama.

The First Time

There comes a time in a young man's life when he has to purchase a particularly embarrassing product. And that time first came for me many years ago. Now in those days, we didn't have self-checkout. And it wasn't a simple thing to drive into another town where you weren't so well-known either. And chances are, some of the local busybodies were hovering around the store, watching for anything that they could gossip about over tea and Fig Newtons. But I had no choice. So with my heart pattering and my face hot, I walked right up to the counter and spoke those dreaded words...

Mr. Calvin, I'm here to pick up my grandma's snuff.

Self-Possessed

My first time living away from home, I moved into a huge, scary, rambling old house. I was absolutely certain it was haunted. One night, as I settled down to a hot bath, I was shocked to see a tub full of...blood. Water should not be any color, especially red. So I ran screaming into the night. My neighbor came over, looked into the bathroom, and smugly explained how the local red clay often gets into pipes and wells and the water sometimes comes out red. He was oh so condescending as he joked about hysterical females and assured me that my house was most definitely *not* haunted.

I cannot tell you how much I enjoyed seeing his reaction to the disembodied face in the mirror and the levitating bed.

Mall Cop

Hey, you can't keep me here; my dad says mall cops aren't real cops.

Sure, I'll tell you what I was doing, just don't get your undies in a bunch.

Me and my best bud Booger were hangin' over the railing, pitching pennies into the fountain down by the food court. Then we figured it would be way cool to aim at a smaller target, like somebody's *head*. How were we supposed to know you were Mr. Undercover Rent-a-Cop?

So why all the drama, Kojak? I'd say that black eye gives you street cred'. You should be thanking us!

Oh yeah, exactly *how* do you think you're gonna get a confession?

(Face starts to contort as he begins to cry like a four-year-old) Nooooo! Don't call my *mom*!

The Crush

Now, calm down; everything's going to be fine. Of course, I love you; aren't you my favorite little cousin?

Let me explain some things to you. Greg wasn't trying to kill me. He wasn't even trying to hurt me. He was just trying to kiss me. See, when I said that Greg has a *crush* on me, well, that doesn't mean he *wanted to crush me.* Saying that someone has a crush on you just means that they like you. So you see, he wasn't trying to crush me or mash me or break me or kill me—just trying to give me a little kiss. You're my hero for trying to save me.

Oh, don't worry about that. Greg will be out of the hospital real soon.

Critter Crisis

You know it could be a lot worse. What if I was bringing home boys with piercings? Or friends with criminal records and tattoos? What if I was associating with *the wrong element*? Why, I could be running around with devil worshipers!

Animals will never steer me wrong or get me into trouble or keep me out late. Okay, I know we've thrown you some curves, like when you found the beaver in the bathtub. And I know Dad was upset when the pigeon pooped in his yogurt. So the ferrets are stealing all the socks and the goat ate up your flower bed. And I'll admit I should have told you I was keeping a garden snake in your underwear drawer. But hey, look at the bright side: we're the only address in the state that's been certified a safe house by the PETA Website!

Parlez-vous?

Wait! Did you just say we have a Spanish test today? We can't be! I'm not prepared! I failed the last cuatro! *(Hold up three fingers as you say "cuatro.")* I think I'm going to faint. No, I'm going to puke. No, I'm going to faint and then puke so I won't know that I puked. I've gotta find a way out of this. Um…I guess I could tell the teacher that I ate a bad jalapeno! *(Mispronounce as Jallah-pee-no.)* Wait, here she comes. I know what I can do—watch this. *(Face the teacher.)* Excusee-mois, senor, yo quito se hablo parakeeto in el testo abuelo de fraulein chipotle? *(Watch as the teacher walks away.)* Gosh, she acts like she doesn't even understand Spanish.

Carsick

What's worse than a long car trip with your brother?

Taking that trip with a little brother who gets carsick.

I know that sounds mean and heartless, but I've spent so much time lately inhaling the stench of recycled fast food that I think it may have affected my brain. And if you think I'm overreacting, just drop by your local Greaseburger drive-through. Oh no—don't go in—go round back to their dumpster and take a whiff.

On this trip, I thought I'd figured it out. I asked Mom to put him in the front seat. I opened my window and stuck my head out, inhaling the fresh air...just as baby brother leaned out the front window and barfed.

Oh, there's nothing like a sixty-mile-per-hour splat.

Dead Wrong

Funerals can be tricky.

I recently attended services for a dear friend. We'd kept in touch by phone and e-mail, but I had not seen her in years. It only took me a little while to get comfortable with her husband and children, and I actually enjoyed talking with her friends and coworkers. We told stories and laughed and cried. I must say, I had some surprises. I found out things about her that I never imagined. And from the looks I was getting, her family was seeing a whole new side of her through my stories and memories.

Finally, I made my exit. Signing the guest book in the foyer, I glanced at the name.

Uh-huh. Wrong funeral.

Touch Up

Excuse me, but I was just wondering if it's possible for you to take my senior picture over again.

See, the entire time you were urging me to smile, smile, smile, you never told me that most of my lunch was caught in my teeth. And I'm not talking about a little bit of spinach hiding behind a molar. We're talking an all-you-can-eat salad bar. With bacon bits and cheese. So I'd really appreciate a do-over.

My dad thought you'd say that, so he told me to tell you this: he runs an advertising firm. If you don't reshoot my pictures, he's going to put my photo on a billboard downtown, saying that this is *your* idea of a glamour shot.

Why, *thank you!* Sure, I'm ready!

Oh, one second—let me check my teeth.

Off-Key

My best friend wants to be a professional singer. And she's the worst singer I've ever heard. Seriously. The worst. It's not just that she's tone-deaf, which she is. Or that she can't seem to pick a key, so she just visits them all. But she only has one volume setting: tsunami. This girl can be heard for miles. She's shattered glass, stopped traffic, and started cattle stampedes. My dog hides when he hears her name, and I think she caused my parakeet's suicide.

But it's her passion. So I can't shatter her dreams.

She says, "Ashley, all my life, I've wanted to sing *so badly.*"

And she does. Oh, she does.

Plus Size

Hey, I'm a big girl.

I thought I'd mention that in case no one has noticed.

I have no problem with my size, so why should anyone else? Actually, I have lots of fun with it. You should have seen the looks when I auditioned for *Project Runway*.

Years ago, there was a commercial on TV that I still remember. Beautiful Jane Russell referred to herself a "full-figured gal." I always liked that. So I think of myself as full: full-figured, full of talent, full of life, and full of love.

I'm forgetting about fad diets and gastric bypass and sweating to the oldies. Like Jane, I'm a full-figured gal and proud of it.

Now, where do I sign up for *America's Top Model*?

Full Disclosure

Before we go out, I think it's my duty to tell you some things about myself.

I have a fondness for plaid shorts and knee socks.

I have relatives who listen to Slim Whitman records.

I believe *The Dukes of Hazzard* is great art and that Pamela Anderson is the next Meryl Streep.

I like to play tennis by myself and solitaire with a partner.

I do not own a computer because I believe covert organizations could see me when I use it.

Plan 9 from Outer Space is the greatest movie ever made.

I refuse to go to McDonald's now that they call it "Mickey D's."

My grandfather will require you to salute and shout, "Long live the Confederacy" before he will allow you on our property.

And I'm absolutely certain that Pee-wee Herman and Marie Osmond are aliens.

So where ya wanna eat?

AWOL

Dear parents,

I'm sending you this video message to let you know what I have learned at camp. First of all, Junior Marine Boot Camp has nothing to do with footwear or sailing. There's no craft hour, so you won't be getting a cool beaded belt or ashtray. There are no games, no cute girls, and no campfire sing-alongs. Just a lot of loud, angry grown-ups with bad breath who yell in your face. I think they're angry because someone made them cut all their hair off.

Did you send me here by mistake? You should really read the brochures a little more carefully in the future.

Please send me a bus ticket or a cake with a file in it.

Love,

Your little soon-to-be AWOL soldier.

Last Gasp

Grandma, why do you make noises when you sleep? Sometimes, you sound like the lawn mower when it won't start and Dad yells at it. And one time, I saw you moving your paws like when the dog is dreaming that he is chasing a squirrel. And then once, your teeth came loose, and I thought they were going to fall out, and I went into the kitchen and put on Mom's oven mitt to catch them if they did, but then you made a smacking sound and they popped back into place. So I was just wondering why you make noises.

Grandma? Grandma, are you sleeping?
Grandma?
Are...you...dead?

Sick Day

(Alarmed; quickly escalating to hysterics.) Oh, no, I am so embarrassed!

Please don't fire me! Please give me a chance to explain!

Okay, I know it was wrong of me to call in sick and then show up at a movie theater, but this isn't just any movie! My boyfriend is a *freak* for *Avatar*. He says I never show any interest in the things he cares about, so I promised him I would see *Avatar* and study it and be able to discuss it intelligently the next time I saw him—which is tonight! Well, I tried to get into every nighttime showing, but they were all sold out, and hey, what was I supposed to do? I don't know the difference between a Na'vi and a Klingon, and this was my last chance to find out what all these blue people were about. So you see, I just had to play hooky today or lose my boyfriend! Oh, please, oh, please, oh, please don't fire me, I—

(Suddenly dead calm.) Um, exactly what are *you* doing here?

Whopper

Fishing is not cool.

When I was little, fishing meant a campfire and eating outside and swimming in the lake.

Then, one summer, my mom said, "Hey, Chelsea, you want to fish with us?" Hey, I just went wading and ate a hotdog—wasn't that fishing? But I went along, and soon the fishing pole was jerking in my hand and everyone was excited. Someone helped me pull the line in. On the end of it was a little fish! He was a baby fish, like the ones in my aquarium. I freaked! I could almost hear the baby fish crying for its mommy! I didn't stop screaming until one of the grown-ups took the fish off the line and put it back into the water and carried me back to the campsite, where I had a nice cold drink and a catfish sandwich.

Oh, Shoot

These are some things my mom told me not to talk about today.

My dad always tells her to lock the front door with her keys so she'll never lock her keys in the house. But she doesn't do it, and she's always locking herself out. So when I hear my mom say, "Oh, shoot," I go around to the back and crawl through the doggie door and let her back in.

My grandma says, "Oh, shoot" too, so I asked her why everybody says, "Oh, shoot" and who am I supposed to shoot when she says that. Grandma says she doesn't mean, "Oh, shoot," but she has to say that because if she says the word she really means, Mom and Daddy won't let her live with us anymore.

Production Problems

Professor Macklin, I want to thank you for allowing me to read your play.

First of all, I think it is very...brave. I think any play that features the reanimated head of Walt Disney is very creative. And I love that you also added Helen Keller and Leonardo da Vinci, but I'm pretty certain they were not alive at the same time. One thing really does confuse me though: you set the play in outer space. I'm thinking it might be less expensive to produce if you just set the play somewhere here on earth.

Oh, I see. It's not *set* in outer space. You will only allow it to be *performed* in outer space.

Ummm...does my grade depend on what I say next?

Seasoned Pro

Stepping into the world of showbiz should be intimidating, but nothing scares me. I've been driving a school bus for twenty-one years.

Do you have any idea how much trouble forty-two kids can get into when there's only one adult in sight, and she has to keep her hands on the wheel? And I have no defense! They took away my taser. And they frown on the use of nerve gas.

I've taken to wearing a football helmet to protect the back of my head. I've pulled gum, taffy, mud, crazy glue, silly putty, silly string, snot, vomit, and a mouse out of the back of my hair.

So bring on the super-agents and very scary casting directors. Unless they assault me with a dead hamster, I look at this as my first vacation in twenty-one years.

Culinary Confession

Stop. Brian, I have waited for you to ask this question from the moment I met you. But before you do, I have to tell you something.

I cannot cook.

No, I don't mean I'm a bad cook. I mean I cannot cook. I have a cease and desist order from the EPA. I once made a chicken salad that was declared a biohazard. My senior home ec project had to be airlifted to an environmental waste dump. Do you know I'm the only short-order cook in history to be fired from a Waffle House? The last place I tried to prepare a meal still has yellow crime scene tape around it.

So go ahead and ask. *(Pause.)* Ask. *(Pause.)* Brian?

Hellhound

Ever see *Cujo?*

That coulda been me—I was trapped by an enraged canine too.

I'd hit the all-night Kroger for some Chunky Munky and left my cell phone at home. No one would be looking for me. No one could save me.

He leapt toward my window just as I got it rolled up. I cried and prayed and tried to get out the other side. But he'd done this before. No matter where I turned, he was waiting with red eyes and monstrous teeth.

Finally, a stray shopping cart bumped against my car. I climbed through the window, into the cart, and paddled my way back into the store, using a broken broom handle and a tree branch. Until I rolled through those automatic doors into the safety of the frozen food section, he was at my wheels, a horror of rippling muscle and snapping jaws.

I'll never look at another Chihuahua the same way!

Control

It's over.

I've tried, but from the moment I brought you home, you have defied and taunted me.

My four-year-old niece can do this, why can't I? I mean, was she born knowing phrases like *server* and *browser* and *webmail?* I still don't know the difference between *ethernet* and *hairnet.* And then when you crashed and took all my files with you, I frantically called the helpline, only to be asked, "Did you back up?" I said *(backing up),* "No, but I'm doing it now—how far?"

So after waiting on you, pampering you, and having you make me feel totally stupid, I'm finally going to do something that I *do* know how to do.

(With glee) I'm pulling your plug.

The Monster

He was sobbing and trembling, almost hysterical. My little boy is only three years old, and I could hardly bear seeing him in this condition. It took a while to calm him down and even longer for him to tell me what was wrong: someone was chasing him. Someone big and dark and scary was following him every step he took. No matter how fast he ran or where he went, this monster was after him. It crept up from behind and hovered over him—a beast without a face.

So I took his hand, and together, we walked out into the world to confront this creature. We found it right away.

My baby boy had discovered his shadow.

Clown Defense

Yes, Your Honor, I did kill him. See, he just stood there smiling at me. No matter what I said, he just smiled and said *(making unintelligible drive-through speaker noises)*. All I wanted was a Happy Burger and Freaky Fries, and that stupid clown just stood there smiling at me with his stupid clown face, making stupid clown noises. I even drove around to the window, but the girl in the window told me I had to go back around and give my order directly into the clown's mouth. She had orange hair and turquoise eye shadow and big red lips, so I think she must have been related to the clown. I drove back around and gave him my order again, but he just said *(more drive-through speaker noises)* and smiled and that's when I snapped and rammed him with my '74 Ranchero. Have mercy. I killed Bozo.

Grand Entrance

Grandma, before we take our seats, let me ask you to do just one thing: please don't embarrass me. The opera crowd is a bit different from your Wednesday night Parcheesi group. They're dignified. Cultured. Do *not* talk to the people onstage. Do *not* fall asleep because your snoring can be heard, I'm sure, above the soprano's dying aria. And for heaven's sake, if you have a problem with gas, please excuse yourself *before* it happens, not after. There are plenty of restrooms if you need to make a stinky.

So. Are we all clear? Dignified? Tasteful? Cultured?

What?

(With the greatest dignity) Yes, I am perfectly aware of the toilet paper hanging out of the back of my dress.

Skinny-Dip

So I'm swimming at the lake with a bunch of my friends. Well, swimming is not exactly the correct phrase—I can't swim. But I had a nice inner tube for floating. I was showing off for Megan when I fell off my tube. No problem, I grabbed it right away. But something felt strange. Different. Missing. Yeah, that's right; my suit had come off in the fall and was nowhere to be seen. And of course, Megan took this moment to paddle right up to me and start talking. I thought about puncturing my inner tube and wearing it as a big rubber swimsuit, but then I would drown. And that would definitely be a turnoff for Megan. So I did what I had to do and exited the lake wearing a tennis shoe, an empty beer can, and a dead trout.

Last Words

Grandma, please wake up. Please don't be dead. Just wake up and I promise I'll never play another trick on you. I'll never again move my mouth without talking, so you think you've gone deaf. I'll confess that I was the one who put Super Glue on your dentures. I'll admit that I was the one who gave your fat little dog Ex-Lax. Please wake up; I can't see you breathing! And, Grandma, I do like your Christmas presents—corn pads and half-empty bottles of Scope are what every boy dreams of! And *I love* your sauerkraut and Fig Newton cakes. I promise I will never ever put cayenne pepper in your enema bag again—

Oh, hi, Grandma.

No, I wasn't saying anything.

You were just dreaming.

Slow Traffic

Just a few minutes ago, I was thinking, *Please, please get the highway clear so I can get through.* But now, inching closer, seeing the blue lights flashing off the wet pavement, I'm just thinking, *Please don't let it be anyone I know.*

The vehicle doesn't look familiar. But then, there's not much left. Calm down. I'd recognize something, wouldn't I? No, doesn't even look familiar. It's a truck. A dark one, black maybe. Do I know anyone with a truck? No one! Not a soul! Wow, that's a relief. And they're letting us through. Careful. Slow. Don't run over any debris. And...I'm...through!

I'm so sorry. Please be all right. You're not someone I know. But someone knows you and is waiting for you to come home. Please be safe. Someone you don't know is thinking about you and sending a prayer your way. Be all right. Please.

Dog House

C'mon, Thumper, please go for Daddy. We go through this every night. I know you have to go. I can practically see you clenching. And I know when you get back in the house, you're going to cut loose. Now, Thumper, you're a big dog. And when you go inside, it pretty much leaves the entire house a toxic disaster zone. I really don't know where it all comes from; I am *not* putting that much in you!

C'mon, boy, just do it. Tell you what; I'll look the other way. Will that help? If you can do it on the Oriental, you can do it in the bushes. If you can do it on the new microfiber sofa (and we both know you can), then you can do it on the lawn. Please?

Okay, I know that look. Let's go back in. But you should know that your mommy's done laid down the law. Betcha me and you both are gonna sleep in the dog house tonight.

Thrill Ride

Carnival rides for little kids give me the willies. It all started with the baby roller coaster. As soon as they strapped me in, I felt something wet. As the cars were pulling out, I realized I was sitting in pee. The ride picked up speed, and I got wetter and colder. Gross. And then there was the Alice in Wonderland Teacups incident. A cup whirled close to me, and I noticed the little girl in it was green in the face. Do you have any idea how dangerous vomit can be on a ride that whirls round in circles? It's like being in a warm, chunky carwash with the windows down. So now I ride the big rides. Sure, they're faster and scarier. But that's okay.

I have learned that adults have much more control over their bodily functions.

Driving Permit

Dad, I know you love me and you're only trying to protect me. But you have to let me get my driver's license. It's not for me. Really. It's for you. It's time you get your own friends. You're scaring mine. The fact that you insist I still ride strapped into my Little Mermaid car seat is just a tad creepy. And I'm afraid the unique sound of your 8-track tape player is totally lost on my friends. And the songs you sing along with—Dad, what does *Boogie Oogie Oogie* actually mean anyway? So let me get my license. I promise not to drive too fast, but, Dad, isn't it possible that you might be driving too slow? Last week, old Ms. Neener passed us in her Hoveround.

Half and Half

My brother and his wife have a new baby. And he's always complaining. I think he's jealous of all the attention that used to go to him. And he says there's never anything in the fridge anymore, either it's full of bottles and baby stuff or his wife pigged out on all the ice cream. So one morning, he's yelling again, head stuck in the fridge, whining that he can't find any milk for his coffee. Finally I hear, "There it is!" and he shuts up. A few minutes later, his wife turns away from the fridge and says, "Honey, have you seen the baby's breast milk?"

I laughed so hard, Cheerios shot out of my nose.

Big Baby

Where does a ninety-seven-pound dog sit?

Anywhere he wants to!

The trouble with our big hound is not that he is ferocious or mean. He's a baby. A really big baby with huge toenails and lots of slobber. And he is afraid of *everything*. Gizmo is scared of doorbells and phones, cartoons on TV, bugs hitting the windows, snow and rain and clouds, my pet hamster Toodles, any song by Lady Gaga (I have to agree with him on that one), and the color yellow. And if he gets really scared, he will (a) pee, (b) jump in your lap, or (c) jump in your lap and then pee.

We really love Gizmo. But then we have to. He's scared of rejection too.

Till Death

See, some people who are—like—married and stuff, they forget how to talk to each other. Sometimes, they even forget why they got together in the first place. And so they just show up every day and eat breakfast with this stranger they don't even know and come home to this person they don't even like. And so they get lonely. And they want to—like—talk, you know, communicate. But they don't know each other anymore, so they just yell. It's the only way they know to reach over across the table. And they yell because they want somebody to remind them who this other angry person is. Or used to be. Or even who they are. Or used to be.

I don't think my parents remember why they got together.

So they yell.

And they yell at me.

So maybe they forgot me too.

Religious Reasoning

I know you told us there was no excuse for not having our homework done. I remember that you said you wouldn't hear any excuses. But you have to hear me out. This is not my fault. In fact, it has nothing to do with me.

The truth is…it's because of my religion. Yes, the reason my homework is not done has nothing to do with laziness or neglect. I *wanted* to do my homework. But I could not go against the religious teachings of my people. I could not disgrace them.

I'm willing to pay the price. Go ahead; punish me for my deep religious convictions if you must.

But hear this first: I gave up homework for Lent.

Toothache

Okay, you said if I could come up with a really good reason why, that I wouldn't have to go to the dentist.

I came up with four!

First of all, you're always saying, "Holly, every time you open your mouth, you get into trouble." *(Shrugs, like, "Doesn't that say it all?")*

Two: What if he gives me truth gas instead of laughing gas, and I start telling family secrets, like where we keep the spare key or that Dad can belch the alphabet or that you sleep with toilet paper wrapped around your hair?

Three: I think the dentist is a pervert and wants to take pictures of me asleep and drooling.

And four *(suddenly crying in desperation):* I have too many teeth! Can't we just let a few of 'em rot away?

Courage

I've dreamed about the Mt. Everest roller coaster at Disney World ever since I was three. I saw some people riding it in a movie, and I just knew I had to get on it. Every time I thought about it, my heart would pound and my hands would shake. But I still wanted to get on it!

Well, I just had my chance. I stood in line with my knees shaking. One by one, they led us toward the cars. A nice lady helped me into the seat, and I was thinking, *This is the last living person I will ever see.* She strapped me in. I closed my eyes and gripped the bar.

So I finally did it. I conquered my fear and got on the Mt. Everest roller coaster.

Next year, I'm actually going to ride it.

The Gap

An apple a day is supposed to keep the doctor away. Too bad it doesn't work on photographers.

The night before our class photos, I decided to chomp into a big yellow apple. I sank my teeth into it—but they didn't come out. That's right, *both* my front teeth stayed buried right down to the core.

Now, I was really little at the time, and it totally freaked me out. I knew my front teeth were loose and that eventually they would come out. But hey, one piece of fruit and I had transformed into my grandmother.

And the next day as I sat in front of the school photographer, and he kept saying, "Smile, little girl, smile," I just glared at him with my mouth firmly closed. Too bad the lights made me sneeze. So I'm forever preserved, eyes squinted shut and granny gums gleaming, in thirty-six mini-prints, twenty-four wallet-size, and one glossy 8 × 10.

Quitting

You have to stop smoking.
No, I don't.
Yes, you do.
How come?
Teacher said so.
So?
You'll get the cancer and die if you don't.
Schoolteachers don't know nuthin'.
I was silent for a moment.
Grandpa?
Huh?
I don't want you to get the cancer.
I won't. Cigarettes don't hurt nobody.
I slid down off the bed, satisfied that my teacher was wrong.
His voice cut sharp through the gloom. Don't you never smoke!
I turned and looked at the back of his head and asked quietly, *Why?*
'Cause it does hurt...girls. It's bad on girls. Promise me you won't never smoke.
I promise.
I turned to leave. In the dim dresser mirror, I watched his reflection as he lit another cigarette. His hands were shaking. I thought he must be cold. I turned back and pulled his shawl closer around his shoulders.
And as I left the room, I thought I heard someone crying.

Drive-Through

I *did* drive up to the first window! Nobody was there, so I drove up here and you told me you couldn't take my money and you couldn't give me my burgers until I paid at the first window, but I've already told you that nobody was there at the first window. Then I drove around and went to the first window, but she told me that I couldn't pay unless I placed my order at the speaker so I promptly drove around *again* and placed my order a second time. But then when I came up to the window to pay, she asked why I was placing my order a second time; that it had already been placed and I needed to go to the second window and pick up my order—so here I am, and now you're telling me that—

Oh, *have it your way,* my aunt Fanny!

I'm going to Taco Bell!

Open Door Policy

Mom, you have to do something about Grammy.

No, it's not her soaps on the TV all day or the fact that she leaves her teeth lying around everywhere. And I'm getting used to the smell of mothballs and Bengay. I don't mind tooth powder in the sink or granny panties hanging on the shower rod.

But, Mom, why can't she shut the door when she's using the bathroom? I'm sixteen years old—this kind of thing could scar me for life! I asked her to shut the door, but she says she doesn't like closed spaces. Says they'll close the lid on her soon enough, she wants some room to breathe while she still can. But, Mom, what about my right to breathe?

On the Paper

Yes, ma'am, I know that is, literally, the oldest excuse in the book. But please read my mom's note again. It doesn't say my dog ate my homework. It says my dog peed on my homework.

See, we're trying to paper-train Bonkers. I'll admit I never should have left my essay lying on the floor. And you can't blame poor Bonky. After all, she *was* going on the paper, so technically, she was doing the right thing.

I know. My mom thought you might not believe me. And she wanted to make *sure* you had proof. So Mom said if you don't believe I really did my homework and that my dog actually peed on it to just say this to you:

Turn the note over.

Personal Space

Would you check out my back please? Any signs back there? Any notes that say, *If you are insane, please approach me immediately?*

What is it about me that attracts nutcases? Why are crazies drawn to me like a magnet? Yes, I am friendly and smile at people. But since when does that mean, "Please leave dismembered Barbie dolls on my front porch?" Yes, I do tend to talk to myself. And I stress I talk to *myself.* I'm not talking to my friend Kapookak from the planet Zardoz, so please don't introduce me to *your* interplanetary acquaintances. And if I should smile at you in passing, please don't start sending me notes made out of letters cut from magazines.

I guess what I'm saying is this: I like people. I don't intend to stop being friendly. But if you don't understand phrases like "inappropriate behavior," "personal space," "stalker," and "restraining order," let me introduce you to my little friend...*Mr. Mace.*

TOTT

Mom, I'm so happy that you finally learned how to text. But please don't—do *not*—ever, ever text *me* again. See, Mom, you cannot just make up your own abbreviations. I mean, how was I supposed to know that IPYLMIYBPPDLI meant "I put your lunch money in your back pocket, please don't lose it!" But the worst part is that you're starting to *speak* in text shortcuts. Mom, you can *text* LOL, but please don't *say* that you were "lolling." And yes, OOH means I am "out of here" when you text it, but to just turn to me when you drop me off at school and say "Oooooh" totally creeps me out.

Face it, Mom, you're just TOTT: too old to text.

Fall from Grace

I fell down the front steps at church.

No one saw me fall. They only saw me as I was attempting to get up. Now, I did not realize at the time how this must have looked: the exiting congregation saw me kneeling before the church, my hands raised heavenward.

They thought I was praying.

It gets worse.

To cover my embarrassment, I pretended to pray as the crowd moved down around me. Then someone saw the blood on my scraped hands and gasped, *Stigmata!*

It gets worse.

But my time is up. If you want to know more, you'll have to read my blog.

Rules of the Road

That is so unfair! All my friends have their driver's license!

I *am* a good driver! I just like doing things my own way. Driving on the left side just feels more comfortable to me. If there's, like, a wasp in the car or something, I'd be able to jump right out onto the side of the road instead of into oncoming traffic—isn't that logical?! And I *do* know how to put it in park before I get out of the car—you just move that thingy up and down those letters that spell PRNDL until the car stops moving. Okay, so when the traffic gets heavy, I do throw my hands over my eyes and scream, "You take the wheel, you take the wheel," but somebody always does, don't they?

Okay, fine, have it your way.

But then, can I have a motorcycle?

Dentity Crisis

I'm having a dentity crisis.

I'm not sure what that is. I think it's like when you have your tonsils out.

I didn't know I had it until I heard my granma telling my mom and dad about it. Granma said, "With all the attention her brothers and sisters get, Katrina must be having a dentity crisis."

At first they said, "No!" but then they said yes. They always say no to granma at first, but then they say yes. So she'll go home.

So I guess they're going to take out my dentity crisis. I'm not scared though. When they took out my tonsils, I got ice cream. When they pull a tooth, I get money.

This thing sounds kinda big.

I'm asking for a pony.

Silly Wabbit

I don't think I can go through with this wedding.

I am so proud to be your maid of honor, but I just don't think I can do it. What if I laugh? No, at this point, I don't think it's a question of whether or not I laugh; it's a question of whether I will laugh so hard that I wet myself.

Seriously, what were you thinking? Okay, I know he married Brandon's parents. And I know they all wanted him officiating over your wedding. But, sweetie, you may as well have Elmer Fudd conducting the ceremony.

I can hear him right now, "Do you, Bwandon, take Bwittany, for your wawfuwwy wedded wife?"

(Pulling it together) No! I can do this. I *will* hold it together.

At least I'll weally, weally twy.

Breakdown

Don't panic. This is a busy road. Somebody will help me. *(Spotting an oncoming vehicle and waving arms wildly)* Oh, hey, can you help me, my car is *(turning body and face as she follows car passing her, then finishing dejectedly)* broken down...

Well, that's okay. Maybe he just couldn't see me. In all this rain.

Oh, goody, here comes a big truck. *(Waving and following the oncoming vehicle with her body and eyes again.)* Hey, hey, can you help me—I need—*(Sudden intake of breath as she is sprayed with water.)* Thanks for the bath, mister!

(Smiling sweetly and waving helplessly at the next car.) C'mon, people, it's obvious I'm a helpless female, and this is my car that's broken down and *(turning into a screaming, angry, wildly gesturing beast as this car passes her too. She's acting just like a serial killer.)* What do I look like, a serial killer?

Wild and Woolly

How can you do this to me? I'm the only person I know whose Mom *hunts!* The kids at school have started calling me Daisy Mae. They think we eat "possum stew" and swim in the "cement pond"!

I mean, it's not like our lives depend on it. Did you know they have this wonderful new invention called the *supermarket?* You can go inside and actually get animals that have already been killed. Do you know how wonderful it would be if you'd just once bring home a meal that didn't still have a face? And you wouldn't always smell like gunpowder and pine needles.

I love you, Mom. But I'd love you more without deer droppings on your shoes and squirrel poop in your hair.

My Debut

Six years old and I had been cast in my first play! I was to portray the role of Bessie Black.

We had a few rehearsals, and I had fun—even though I had no lines. And for some reason, I had to follow Gracie Birdwell everywhere she went. I must be playing Gracie's sister or best friend.

And then came dress rehearsal. Turns out I was not playing Bessie, but Bossie. And it wasn't Bessie Black, it was Bossie's back. Yes, I was the rear end of a cow and spent the entire play stuffed in a smelly cow suit and staring at Gracie's large behind.

Just telling you this to let you know how easy I'll be to work with. After my debut as a cow's butt, I'll be grateful for anything.

The Naked Truth

At night, my mom takes off her false eyelashes and hairpiece.
My dad has contact lenses that turn his eyes blue.
My granpa keeps his false teeth in a jar and my granma has over twenty wigs.
When our neighbor lady goes jogging, my big brother says the only thing real about her is the twinkle in her eye.
And they say to me, "Lindsey, always tell the truth."
(Pause) I am *so confused.*

Repeat

Mom, please, please don't be mad at Wilbur!

Well, I think he ate the cake that you made for Uncle Jack's birthday. Because he has frosting on his whiskers and paws. And he was chewing on a big number 41 candle when I found him. But he spit the candle out, so you can still use it. And I don't think Uncle Jack will want his present either. Because well…Wilbur barfed on it, and now it's all shriveled and covered with drool and sprinkles.

But Mom, I know the cake was really yummy. Because after Wilbur barfed it up—he ate it again!

The Big Reveal

Mom, just stay outside the dressing room.

I know I've waited till the last minute. But, Mom, this is my dream prom dress. It's the right color and size and—well, it wasn't *exactly* my size. So I figured I'd make it work. And I did until that last little tug when it caught in my underwear. And when I tried to get it loose, well, now I'm standing here in a ruined prom dress and shredded undies. Please help me out of this, and I promise I'll never wait till the last minute again. And *please* don't let anyone know about this—I would *die of embarrassment!*

Okay, stand back. I'm opening the door.

(With as much dignity as possible) Hello. Would one of you please stop laughing and go find my mom?

End of Patients

Ma'am, can a doctor see me now?

I think this *is* an emergency; that's why I'm in the emergency room.

Well, I can't walk, my head is bleeding, and should anyone's arm really be *this many* colors?

I already gave you that information, but okay…

I was hit by a fat man while snow tubing.

Yes, I know snow tubes are soft. But I wasn't hit by the tube. I was hit by the man. He must have been too heavy for the tube, the tube exploded, and he kept going.

No, I think he's fine. I must have cushioned the blow. But thanks for asking about him; your concern is noted.

Yes, he was really fat.

How fat exactly?

About your size but with a smaller moustache.

Orphan

Please don't pick me up at my house. I'll meet you there.

No, I'm not ashamed of you. It's just that my family is... If anyone comes over, Dad starts in on one of his theories, like how birds nurse their babies and it's entirely possible to milk them. And if a boy comes over, my mom does a puppet show about celibacy using broccoli, snow shoes, and a vacuum cleaner. My brother has arguments with my sister, except that I don't have a sister. My dog is scared of the phone and he has gas; we dread getting phone calls.

So it's not that I'm ashamed of my family, it's just...

Can I come live with you?

Perfect Date

Dad, please let him take me to the prom! He is the coolest guy at our school!

Okay, his name is Bobby, but *please* don't call him that. Call him Belch or Stain. And if you forget what to call him, remember it's tattooed on his neck. He's got the greatest car I've ever seen—he had the doors removed so you don't have to hang out the window, you just...*hang out!* And his hair is *amazing;* it's totally white with a long orange ponytail that he wears over one eye. Oh, and please don't make him talk too much. He's got a tongue piercing that's still healing.

Dad, why are you unlocking the gun cabinet?

Dad?

Old Pro

When I was just a kid, I auditioned for my first show. It was *Charlie and the Chocolate Factory.* I went crazy when I got the call that I was cast as this guy called Oompa. Oompa Loompa. I asked the lady on the phone if that was a big part. She said, "Oompa Lompa's everywhere—all over the stage and in almost every scene."

Score! My first audition and I got the lead. Then I showed up for rehearsal and almost every little kid in the room said they were playing my part.

I was ready to throw some punches when a big kid explained that Oompa Loompas were the little worker guys. I was just part of the crowd!

Showbiz is *tough.*

First Take

I've already made my film debut.

A few years ago, I was touring Warner Brothers Studios. I broke away from my group to visit the ladies' room. When I returned, I didn't notice that I was following a different group; I just thought we'd acquired a new tour guide. He was very rude and ordered us about.

Suddenly, we were herded to an ordinary looking street and told to run from this point *(pointing far to the left)* to this point *(pointing far to the right)* when we saw the first explosion. And before I could process what was happening, the chaos began.

So if you ever happen upon an episode of *Smallville* in which a neighborhood is pummeled with Kryptonite, look for me. I think you'll find my fit of hysteria quite believable.

Turkey Tale

We took a long trip for Thanksgiving to see a grandmother I had never met before. She tried to hug me, but it was like, who is this strange person grabbing at me? Everything was different at her house, even the food. I told them I wasn't going to eat my grandmother's strange food. Her cranberry sauce had cranberries in it. And the dressing was *inside the turkey!* So I wouldn't eat until my mom told me that she had really made the turkey and the cranberry sauce at home and just brought it all with us. Then after I ate it, my mom told me that my grandmother really made it after all, and everybody laughed at me.

I felt so betrayed.

Stalled

(Normal speed)   Don't yell; this could have happened to anybody!

(Very fast)   See, I was in the dressing room at the Gap and Megan was in the next stall, and I wanted to give her a little scare, so I pulled a stocking cap over my face and slid under the stall. Just as she turned around, I said, "Hey, baby, what's shakin'" in a really deep voice. Megan looked down, but instead of freaking out, she pepper sprayed me, but some of it must have got in her eyes, and she fell and knocked herself out. *But* she fell against the door she was trying to open, and the door pinned me by the neck in the corner on the floor, and she passed out against the door, and I couldn't move and nobody could get the door open because she was passed out against it. When they found us, I was squashed on the floor in a stocking cap, and Megan was dead to the world with a bra on her head.

(Normal speed)   See, it could have happened to anybody.

Couple

Okay, I'll admit that I don't hate that we're a couple. For now. And I figured I'd seen it all, but you did throw me a few curves. Like, I've always been the daddy. I never had anyone take care of me. Oh, a few have tried, but it just didn't feel...right. It wasn't comfortable for me. I guess it put into question my own definition of who I was, who I am. But when I've had it, when I'm down, when I'm small and weak, you know just what I need—even if it's just space. Other times, you lay down beside me and I feel, well, protected. Home. Safe. Small. And happy to be so.

So I guess what I'm saying is that I think you did the right thing, just pushing your way into my life and becoming a part of it. If you'd asked me, I never would have let you. But you didn't ask. You knew.

Now, get your leash and let's go out for a run. But no barking at squirrels!

Perfect Fit

Fine. I'll answer your questions, but then you have to answer a question for me.

First, yes, you look great in that dress. The color is just right, and I like the way the little flowers in the pattern bring out your eyes. I think you could have it let out a little in the hips though. Sorry, but you are a little wide in the butt and that dress shows it up. And the neckline—are you sure you want it that low? Maybe you could wear it with a scarf or a camisole. But overall, yes, you look really great in that dress.

Now my turn: why is my fifteen-year-old brother wearing a dress?

No Picnic

Please don't leave, Aunt Nooney. We love you, and we look forward to seeing you at the family picnic every year. But we can't eat your potato salad. The truth is, we haven't been eating it for years. We just ran out of ways to get rid of it. We used to dump it under the table, but it burned the grass and left holes in the ground. Then we put it in the park trash cans, but the ranger said it was killing the squirrels. I took it home one year and flushed it, but it dissolved our pipes.

Maybe you could just change the recipe. See, most potato salad doesn't crunch or make your gums bleed. And I really don't think it should have anything blue in it.

What? Bring your sauerkraut cake instead?

Hey, pass me some of that potato salad!

Screenplay

Stage fright? Me? I've already made my film debut, and nothing can scare me now.

See, my husband was determined to record the birth of our first child.

For weeks he talked about camera angles, and I talked about hairstyles. He considered lighting difficulties, and I fretted over what to wear.

Well, after fourteen hours of labor, I lay in a pool of sweat, hair in my eyes, and dingy hospital gown nearly torn to shreds. I was hoarse from screaming, and I was thinking that my eyes might *literally* bug out of my head. I had called my husband words I did not know I even knew and hurled at him every object within reach.

Stage fright? *(Looking around happily.)* Hey, this is nothing. And I even get to do this one standing up!

Walking Disaster

My friends say that I'm a walking disaster. I'll just say that gravity is not my friend.

I have fallen down stairs and up stairs. I tripped on flat ground and slipped on dry pavement. I steered a bicycle into a brick wall and once entered a store through their show window. Falling down an escalator, I took everyone else with me. You've heard of actors falling off the stage, but I somehow managed to fall *on*stage. From the orchestra pit.

So you may be thinking, I should really avoid this girl. No. Don't think of me as dangerous. I mean, what else could happen to me? Think of me as *pre-disastered.*

(Walk carefully and very slowly offstage.)

Brothers

I was raised in a houseful of older brothers. It's safe to say, it took me a while to get in touch with my feminine side.

I hear that a young sister is often spoiled by her brothers and treated like a little doll. I was treated more like a football. Yep, we have family pictures of baby Nancy being used as a paperweight, as third base, and as a tie-down for Stinky the dog.

Then I got older and we got into the hand-me-downs. I don't mean to paint a sad picture, but my first prom dress was corduroy.

It's worth it, though, when you consider all the good things that come from being raised in a family of boys.

And when I think of some, I'll get back to you.

Parting Words

I am so proud of you! My big sister is getting married!

You look so beautiful. The gown is perfect with all the yards and yards of white silk and satin.

I hear the music starting. Before you go, I have three very important things I want to say to you.   And I want them to be the last thing you hear from me before you start down the aisle. So I'm going to stand right here beside the door. I'll say them, then I will leave. *(Start to make your way offstage, as if leaving the room.)*

First, I love you very much.

Second, thank you so much for allowing my little dog Scooter to come to the wedding. You know it means so much for me to have him with me.

And finally *(getting ready to dash off),* I want you to know…you sat in dog poop. *(Run offstage.)*

Leak-proof

How do you tell your mom it's time for adult diapers? And no, I'm not making fun of her because she is old or has a medical condition. In fact, she has the constitution of a camel. She can sit through a Hugh Jackman movie marathon after drinking three iced teas and a Big Gulp. What she has is more of a...*giggle condition.* See, whenever she laughs, she *(making a "you know" gesture with hands).* So when she watches a funny movie or jumps on the trampoline or hears a funny joke—well, you get the idea. And the worst part is, when she does *(making the "you know" gesture again),* it makes her laugh and she does it again, which makes her laugh again...

Look, Mom, all I'm saying is, we potty trained the baby and paper trained the dog. So if you'll pardon the expression, maybe it's time for you to go with the flow.

Scrapbook

Mom, stop with the pictures. I know you are proud of me, but not every girl I go out with wants to see a picture of me when I was just an hour old. I look like a hobbit. And I know you think my little three-year-old bottom was cute, but did you have to document every moment of my naked phase?

And the slumber party pictures? So what if a guy has a crush on his older sister's girlfriends? So what if I let them dress me up? So what if I did join in their fashion shows and lip-synch contests? It was the only way they'd let me stay. So please, Mom, no more pictures. Let's face it: it can be a real turnoff to see your boyfriend dressed as Mariah Carey.

Dirty Secrets

Mom. Mom! *Mom!*

(Quietly, a private thought only) Oh, no, please don't tell him about it. Please! These things are taken care of. You don't need to—

Mom!

(Quietly) Oh, you're not going to listen to me. You're going to go right ahead and tell him all about it.

No, no, Mom, that's not who you think it is!

(Quietly) I can't believe you're saying that to him. Please let this just be a nightmare. *(Defeated.)* No, it's not a dream. She just did it. Right here in front of everybody.

Uhmmm…Mom? Thanks for announcing in front of the entire parent-teachers' association that I just threw up in the hall. And that little man that you just sent off to clean up the vomit? That wasn't the janitor. That's our new principal.

Humor in Uniform

Hello, Officer.

Oh, I have no idea; I never really look at the speedometer.

Driver's license? Now, what exactly would that look like, and do you have any idea where I might find it?

Proof of insurance? Hey, I'm pretty sure I don't have any insurance. So I guess it would be pretty hard for me to prove it, now wouldn't it?

Ticket? Oh, no, thanks, I don't think I would. Because, see, I have a whole collection of them right here in the glove box. But thanks for asking.

Do I think I'm funny? Not really, but my friends do.

You know what might cheer you up? Getting a little color in your wardrobe. All that dark blue—why, it's practically a uniform.

(Pause) You're not what most people would call a laugher, are you?

High School Confidential

I woke up late for school. Of course, I'm out of clean underwear, so I put on a pair of my brother's. Hey, desperate times...

I hurried off to school, burst through the doors, raced down the hall, and found the classroom empty. I think that's when it hit me that it was Saturday.

Okay, no problem. I head back toward the door, only to find it padlocked. Apparently, the janitor had just finished and locked up. I found a phone and called the police, but before they could arrive, I became hysterical, broke open a window, cut myself, and passed out. Not able to find the source of the blood, paramedics take off my clothes and reveal that I'm apparently a cross-dressing hemophiliac.

That would have been bad enough if that story happened when I was a student. But no. I was the teacher.

Leaving the Nest

I think it's time you moved out.

Now, before you say anything, let me finish. Everyone has to leave home at some point and start their own life. This will be good for you. You've become completely dependent on me cooking and cleaning for you. You have to learn to do things for yourself. And you need to make some friends your own age. All you do is watch TV, text, play computer games, and surf the Internet. Get out into the world and get a life! I guess what I'm saying is, I love you, but it's time you get up, get out, and get a life of your own.

It's time for you to grow up.

Now, what would you like for lunch today, Mom?

Sleep Disorder

(Calling through the bedroom door) Dad, I hate to wake you up, but you've got to stop snoring so loudly!

Dad, can you hear me? It's really getting bad. You remember that scene in *Jurassic Park* when they could tell that the T-Rex was approaching 'cause the liquid in the cups started to vibrate? Last night, you vibrated water out of the upstairs toilet. Dad? Can you hear me over the roar? It's not just us anymore. The neighbors are starting to complain that you're interfering with their cable reception. Planes are having trouble landing, Dad, you're starting to show up on radar! My friends won't pick me up at home; they call you "The Amityville Snorer"!

(Practically screaming) Dad, you've got to stop snoring and wake up!

(Looking to the side with shock and surprise) Dad?

(Looking back to the bedroom door in horror) Mom!

Driving Test

You're *what?* You're failing me? I've waited fifteen years to get my driver's license, and you're telling me you can just—*not give it to me?*

What did I do wrong? I know I hit every one of those orange cone targets—knocked 'em all down! And I made it through all the intersections—even the ones with red lights. And I didn't let any of those crazy people screaming from the roadside distract me. And that cardboard cop on the obstacle course—didn't I flatten him?

I don't think you should be giving driving tests anyway. It's obvious you're afraid of cars. Did you know you were sweating the entire time I was driving and your face was white? I think I even heard you praying a couple of times.

If you're so afraid of cars, you should really get into some other business.

Q&A

Good morning, class. Let me address the following notes that were left on my desk yesterday.

Brittany, incorrect. That is not George Jefferson on the one-dollar bill.

Norbert, I agree with you. The fact that the Democrats and Republicans are parties is probably the reason nothing ever gets done.

Ivan, your dad can help you with your homework, even though he did not go to the same school. Surprisingly, math is taught almost everywhere.

Avery, if this question is still valid, yes, you may go to the restroom. And please hurry.

Maria, no, there is not a lot of noise in Illinois.

Trevor, while it is true that people from Poland are Poles, it is *not* true that people from Holland are Holes.

And finally, thank you, Zac, but it couldn't possibly be on crooked because it is not a wig.

Mount Vesuvius

Yes, I know why I'm here. I knew I'd end up in the principal's office. I mean, after the explosion and all...

See, I read the directions wrong. I was supposed to put *baking* powder in the volcano, and then add the vinegar to make it explode. But I couldn't find any baking powder, so I just went out to my dad's garage and used *gun*powder instead. I mean, they're both *powder,* see? So I thought that would be okay.

And you have to admit, it did explode!

So yes, I know why I'm here, and I'm sorry about the windows in the science room, and I'm sorry about the hamster. And I hope Ms. Tilly gets out of the hospital real soon.

And, Principal Terry...I think you look just *fine* without eyebrows.

Little Demons

Kids turn evil when I babysit them.

I know what you're thinking: Once Mommy and Daddy leave the house, the little darlings start to misbehave, testing the babysitter to see how far they can go.

If only.

No, I recently watched one little cherub actually grow horns and a forked tail as soon as we heard the parents' car drive away. They bite, scream, fight, destroy, tear, scratch, and bellow. I would not be surprised to see one of them spew green pea soup and levitate.

And the damage is not just limited to the house. I've answered the door to find they've ordered everything from pizza to a stripper. Okay, so I kept the pizza.

But my biggest problem is not just trying to survive the night—it's explaining to the parents what has happened to their home and offspring. Little Ana cut off her sister's hair, and Bobby colored his blond curls with a permanent black magic marker. Megan superglued the cat to the curtain, and Zachary superglued— well, let's just say I now carefully check toilet seats.

So, dear parents, if you are finding all the babysitters are refusing to do return engagements, may I suggest something?

Hire an exorcist next time!

Pleather

Could you please seat us somewhere else? No, it's not the location; isn't that *pleather*? See, restaurant booths are made out of pleather. Pleather splits. I can't sit on anything pleather. When these seats split, you can see the white fuzzy stuffing underneath. I think that might be the gateway to hell.

When I was little, I saw an episode of *The Twilight Zone* where a little girl rolled off her bed and was sucked into another dimension. And all around her was this gauzy, cottony stuff. Then one day, I was sitting on a kitchen chair when the pleather split, and I saw that stuff gaping below me and I was sure I was going to be sucked in.

Oh, thank you; this table is much nicer.

Wait! Isn't that...*(with the same horrified reading as "pleather")* formica?

OMG!

My parents just put restrictions on my cell phone! They said I am texting too much!

OMG, how am I supposed to communicate with my BFF Lindsey? Texting too much? Oh, I am LMBO! And BTW, I think my parents are just jealous, because IMHO, I don't think they even *know how to text*—LOL! My mom says that 13,000 messages a month is entirely too much—but how would she know what's too much? She only uses her phone to *talk* and still thinks cell phones give you brain tumors. LMBO, and she still thinks cell phones give you brain tumors. *(Appears vaguely confused, then clutches pocket.)* Oh, NM—text message coming in. G2G now. Too much texting? They must be JK.

TTYYL! Smiley face, smiley face!

Safe

My brother is a disaster area. I love him, but he should be surrounded by yellow crime-scene tape. If you get close to him, better make sure your insurance is paid up. My brother can trip over thin air. He spends so much time in the emergency room that they're giving him his own wing. During his time with a marching band, he marched into a stop sign, a city bus, a parked train, and a slow-moving cow. He once put wasp spray on his armpits and has used Super Glue as hair gel and Preparation H as toothpaste.

He's here with me today. But don't worry, I took precautions. He's the guy sitting near the back—duct taped to his chair.

Help Line

Hello, *Rooms 2 Go Kids* help line? I'm shouting because the phone is on the wall across the room, and I had to lift the receiver off and dial the number with a sponge mop. No, actually, I think it was a Swiffer. So that wouldn't be a sponge mop really, it would be a—oh, never mind—I need help!

See, I bought this high chair for my little niece. And when I put it together, it didn't look very safe. See, the only thing holding Darlene in is the tray! So I just decided to test it myself. Only I didn't want to try it from the outside, so I got into the high chair and pulled the tray shut towards me and—yes, ma'am, I am an adult. Yes, ma'am, it was a little tight. Yes, ma'am, I am now fully satisfied that the tray will not accidentally disengage, allowing my niece to fall! Hello?

He-hello?

The Mouths of Babes

Gramma, when my sweaters get all stretched out and saggy, my mom puts them in the dryer, and they draw up and fit me again. So I was thinking maybe you should get Mom to put your skin in the dryer. Then it wouldn't be so saggy and wiggle when you move around.

And, Gramma, did they have the tooth fairy when you were a little girl? 'Cause I was just thinking that if they did, you probably got about a million dollars for all your missing teeth.

And, Gramma, how come every time I ask you questions, all you say is, "Child, you ain't right."

Improv

What do you do when you forget your lines onstage?

(Inhale, start to speak, and then look off, totally lost. Then) Oh yeah, I got it now. *(Speaking very fast.)* What-do-you-do-when-you-forget-your-lines-onstage? *(Speaking normally again.)* Well, my coach tells me to just keep going. No matter what, don't stop. Just...keep going. Just say something. Anything. Just go on and on and on until...I got it! Just don't panic; that's right! Just think about the subject you're talking about, and then, even if you can't remember your next line, whatever you say will make sense because it's on the right subject.

Just remember...the subject....what the scene is about...what it's about...

(Turning and starting to leave. To herself) I had this; I so had this. It was something about...um, about...umm...

Hall Monitor

Excuse me, mister, all visitors to our school have to wear a name tag.

You have to go down to that door at the end of the hall. That's the principal's office. When you go in, sit very quietly and wait until someone tells you what to do. Do not talk. If you think you want to talk or laugh real loud or scoot your chair on the floor to make a poopy sound, just don't do it. Listen to the angel that sits on your right shoulder and don't listen to the devil that sits on your left shoulder. Oh, and don't stare at Ms. Wilson's moustache either or tell her that she should shave it off. Boy, I learned that one.

(Listens for a moment) Okay, then go tell her that's your name, and she'll give you a name tag that says "Mister Superintendent of Schools."

Missing the Beat

Please Dad, don't dance. Don't ever dance. Don't dance if they offer you money. Don't dance if your life depends on it. Don't dance if *my* life depends on it.

I don't want to hurt your feelings. I just want to save our family from decades of humiliation and shame. You are, without a doubt, the worst dancer in the history of the world. In fact, I don't think it's really dancing. It's more like the death throes of an injured jungle beast. You say you can dance like Fred Kelly or Gene Astaire, but I don't even know which group those guys are with.

So please, Dad, just hitch up your Sansabelt slacks and enjoy your old age. I know you think you're a Backstreet Boy, but, Dad— *you're thirty-five!*

Flushed

What do you mean you can't fix the sewer pipe? It says so right on your truck, right under *We Fix Anything* and *Let Us Flush Your Troubles Away.* And until you *do* flush my troubles, there will be no flushing! I'm having a New Year's party tonight! What are my guests supposed to do—hold it? That pipe is emptying right into my basement, and unless you do something right now, by New Year, we're going to be in deep—*trouble.* Now, I don't care whether you replace the pipe or work a minor miracle with duct tape or just stand downstairs with your hand on the pipe and pray for healing, but you are not leaving this house, fella, until this is fixed. I'm an angry housewife on a budget—don't mess with me, mister.

Anne Frank

I thought it would be bigger. I wanted it to look like the movie. I wanted it to be a movie. But it's real. And so very small.

Did this space ever become home to you? Did you ever call this "my room"? Or was it always just a place to hide? Did you ever feel safe here?

Sometimes, I forget that you were just a little girl. Not today, though. Right now, standing in your room, I can imagine you, frail and dark, spending your hours in this little space, dreaming of all the things little girls do.

Someone is coming up the stairs now. You listened to footsteps climb those very stairs on that last night.

Wherever you dwell today, I hope you somehow sense that you made this world a better place.

This little room still looks so small. But it holds a grand spirit. I feel better now. Thanks for listening. Be at peace, Anne.

Little Voices

Honey, Mama loves you, but you gotta go to bed before Preacher gets here. Because last time, you asked the preacher's wife why her chest has a butt crack. And you shouldn't have told her Mama ran outta clean underwear and was wearing Daddy's. And I know you meant no harm, but I'd rather you hadn't told the preacher that Daddy says his sermons are better than a Sominex. No, you shouldn't tell them when they have food in their teeth *or* a booger in their nose, and you shouldn't repeat Daddy when he says things like his mother-in-law is meaner than Satan and older than God. No, you don't need to ask them how many poos they made today.

Honey, you know how Mama always told you to speak up like a big boy? Mama was *wrong.*

Gutter Ball

He said he would teach me how to bowl. I said he couldn't. I sat quietly, feeling my Mountain Dew cup sweating into my hand. Suddenly, I was up! My macho boyfriend stood behind me pushing and yelling and criticizing and booming instructions. "Just do it!" he yelled from behind me. So I dove down the alley, throwing my arm backwards with all my might. When I drew my arm forward, it was considerably lighter. I guess I didn't get all the sweat from my drink cup off my hands. I looked around for the ball. And my boyfriend. I found him sorta crumpled on the floor with the bowling ball between his legs. He spent the rest of the night in the corner with popsicles from the snack bar piled in his lap. The doctor says he'll be walking again soon. And every time I mention bowling now, he starts to cry.

Just Desserts

I smell it.

She did it again. I don't think I can go through this anymore. Why don't you tell her? If it was my grandmother I'd tell her. I'd say, "Meemaw, I don't want to hurt your feelings, but I'd prefer not to eat any more of your disgusting bread pudding."

Not that bad?

First of all, I don't think turtle is a traditional ingredient in any dessert. I swear it tried to crawl off my plate on Sunday. And then there was the time I found a sponge curler in my portion. Last month when she said she'd lost her dentures, I nearly gagged.

I just can't eat it again! If you don't tell her—I will!

(Big smile) Meemaw! *Mmmmmm...* is that bread pudding I smell?

Plain or Chunky?

I gobbled my peanut butter sandwich, grabbed a bench by the jogging path, and let my pretty smile and pretty words work for me. Every young lady who passed by was finer than the last one, and I waved and nodded. And they laughed. And laughed. Why are they laughing? So I tried my surefire killer smile on the next one. *(Giving a big studly grin.)* And she laughed so hard, she blew some tutti-frutti Big Gulp out her nose. The next one got my smoldering, sexy look. *(Giving a smoldering, sexy look.)* And she cracked up! Then she turned back and said, "Good luck, Skippy!" Skippy? Oh yeah, that's right—leftover peanut butter all *over* my face and nuts in my teeth!

Color-Blind

I've always believed that love is blind, and now I know it. I was getting ready for a big date. He was sweet, tall, and dreamy. The fact that he was Caucasian was just a minor feature—no biggie. I picked out the perfect outfit and bought an expensive new facemask. When I removed it—there's no other way to say it—I was white. I was just a black girl with a white face. As I reached for the doorknob, my heart was pounding. Would he think this was a joke? A racial comment? Or would he just think I was an idiot. As it turned out, I have no idea what he thought. I only know how he treated me: like a princess. He smiled at me—at my ridiculous face—and never once acted as if anything was wrong. Yes, love is blind. And the best kind is also color-blind.

Hot Flash

Grandma, we love having you here. Even Dad. He only complains because, Grandma, this isn't Florida. We know you're used to the hot weather down there, but maybe you could make some adjustments that aren't related to keeping the thermostat at 114 degrees. Have you ever noticed how we're wearing coats this winter? Everyone does! And we wear shoes around the house. And even socks! I know you love your flip-flops and sundresses, but they just won't cut it up here. How about if we compromise: wear a sweater over your tube top and socks with your sandals. You could start a new fad! And Dad wouldn't go into cardiac arrest when the heating bill comes in. And I wouldn't be sweating through my sheets in winter. And one more favor, Grandma—for you, for me, for all of us—please close your robe.

Family Affair

What's the best way to bond with your family? Well, it's not camping during a cold snap in a broken-down camper near a lake where all the fish had just died and washed up on shore. Our rented camper, which I swear had seen Civil War duty, broke down on the highway. Arriving late at the lakeside, we finally bedded down and I fell into a coma—uh—I mean, deep sleep. About 4:00 a.m., I hear a steady *knock-knock-knock* on the camper's flimsy door. Not knowing whether to expect Freddie Kruger or Jason Voorhees, I flung open the door wearing my wife's shorty kimono and brandishing what I thought was a knife, but revealed itself to be a Barbie Doll. It was my son, who had fallen onto the ground through a hole in the camper floor. Right behind him was the dog, who had also fallen through, but had taken the time to roll in the dead fish before bouncing back into the tiny trailer. And yet after all this, our kids said, "When can we go again, Daddy?"

Don't you just hate kids?

Pampers

Have you seen the new exploding diapers? Oh yeah, apparently my mom uses them.

My baby brother is fretting in church, so my mom slips out. When she comes back, she hands me a small bundle. Now, why she brought it back with her, I do not know. And to this day, I don't remember clapping or shifting in my seat or even moving at all. I just know that the bundle in my hand exploded. I screamed. The preacher must have thought I was moved by the Holy Spirit because he pointed right at me.

My nickname at church now is Pampers.

Thanks, Mom.

Last Lesson

I used to think that people grew up as they grew older. Not true. Some people have tiny little kid-brains trapped in an adult's body. Case in point: my old third-grade teacher. Seeing her again last week made me feel just the way I did when I was in her class: I wanted to throw up. It's not just that she's ugly—which she is. Or that she is old as dirt—which she is. But she's really mean. If one student acted up, she'd punish the whole class. One time, I stayed up all night working on a project she had given me at the last minute. I think I was fighting to get her approval, but she flunked me anyway. And she has absolutely no sense of humor. Which is surprising, considering how she dresses. She really seems to despise young people. And that makes me question why she became, of all things, a teacher. I think maybe she wanted to be a teacher so she could have some control over others. But seeing all these young people so full of life just makes her more angry and bitter.

So in conclusion, I believe that being an adult is not something that just happens automatically as you get older. I think it's something that you have to earn.

Well, it looks like the old bat taught me something after all.

Royal Flush

I hope this doesn't embarrass you, but...well, if I'm brave enough to tell it, you should be brave enough to listen. I'm talking to my boyfriend on my cell when suddenly I have the overwhelming urge to use the ladies room. I mean, it is a *mobile phone,* and I can be very careful and quiet and—no problem. Well...big problem. Everything's going fine until I turn to flush, and the phone slips from between my chin and shoulder and—*ker-plunk*! I plunge my hand into the—uh—water, all the while shouting to my boyfriend as if he's the one drowning. "C'mon, Josh, c'mon, baby!" I try everything, including mouth-to-mouth. But it was over.

And there you have it: another relationship down the toilet.

Freshman

I saw you. I saw you walk past the cool table with your lunch tray held steady and your eyes ahead. I saw you when the cheerleaders whispered and giggled as you passed. And I definitely saw you when you changed direction, slipped on that pat of butter, and sent your tray and its contents high up toward the ceiling lights. And I saw when your legs went up into the air, and you seemed to hang, hang for just a second, before you were showered with peas and corn and Apple Brown Betty. And I laughed. Just like everyone else. I laughed. I mean, c'mon, you just sat there in your mashed potatoes with a corn muffin on your head. So I laughed. But then I decided I had to come and find you. Hey, I was a freshman once too.

Hoodlums

Some guys my age like to race cars; some others race motorcycles. Billy and I like to race golf carts. They may not be as fast and they may not be as cool, but they're a *lot* more fun when you flip them. One time, we had just finished a huge shaving cream fight—but that's another story—and we were speeding across a parking lot in our golf carts. All of a sudden, this guy comes running at us, waving his arms, and screaming. We slowed down, but he kept coming at us, yelling and pointing. As he got closer, we could hear him yell, "Jump the hole! Jump the hole!" He was pointing at a huge pothole! We had thought we were in trouble, but this guy just wanted to see us jump the carts over the pothole! And this guy was really old too! I mean…like *thirty*.

Power Mower

I hate to mow the lawn. It's not very feminine. And it's not very dignified. Things *jiggle,* and there's nothing you can do about it. Finally, my excuses didn't work anymore, and my dad said I *had* to cut the lawn. "The universe will punish you for this!" I yelled. "Just be expecting it. The universe will punish you!" No gypsy curse ever sounded better. I fired up the mower and started to cut. Almost immediately, we heard a high-pitched sound, a whir, then a crash. The windshield on Dad's brand-new Lexus was totally shattered. And before he could even think about murdering me, he found in the front seat—a golf tee *he* had left on the lawn.

Oh yeah…I am *scary.*

Tomorrow

Nobody talks to you. I've never heard you speak. I don't think I even remember a teacher calling on you in class.

You're the girl in the back. Small. Faded. Forgotten.

Why do they avoid you? Is it because your clothes look worn? Because you hold your head down and clutch your books too close? Because they sense some sadness about you that they might catch, catch like a bad cold? Or is it because...because they could be you? With a lost job or a long illness, their family could be stretching money too far and wearing outfits too long. Dad misses a paycheck, and their skin treatments and manicures would be a thing of the past.

I'll talk to you. I'm not afraid of you.

What could they be thinking? Why won't they talk to you?

Well, I will. I'll talk to you.

Tomorrow.

Stop Sign

I suppose it's human nature to try to get out of a traffic ticket. But that stop sign wasn't there before—I knew it! I had driven this road for years, and there was never a stop sign! But the officer was so convincing that I was beginning to doubt my own sanity. It seems he lived nearby, and he told me that sign had been there for twenty years. Finally, I gave up the fight. There was nothing to do but take the ticket, pay it, then go have my eyes checked. Just as he was finishing the paperwork, a DOT truck pulled to a stop. "Hope there's no problem with that stop sign already," a voice called from the cab, "we just put it in last night!"

The man in the truck waved and pulled away. The cop never looked at me. He walked in a very dignified manner back to his car. He got inside, pulled off, stopping politely at the new stop sign with the fresh dirt around the post. Then he drove off very slowly into the distance; the brake lights on his squad car almost as red as his face.

Bathroom Break

I am so sorry. My wife said she coming up here to use the bathroom. I just thought I'd hide in the shower and jump out and— oh, I know it sounds stupid, but she likes it in the bathroom. I mean—when I'm in the bathroom—I mean—when I scare her, well, not scare her, just—I am so sorry. I didn't see anything. Not that there was anything to see! And I wanted to give you some privacy, so I put my fingers in my ears but I could still hear. You. Going. And so I thought I'd just hum to block out the noise—I know that was dumb, but I was getting claustrophobic and having a panic attack! I can't stop thinking about how awful that must have been for you to be sitting there with *When the Roll Is Called Up Yonder* coming from behind the shower curtain.

I'll shut up now.

Little Sister

Katrina, when you were born, I thought you were the sweetest little baby sister in the whole world. And you were so very pretty. I heard "Will you just look at all that *hayer?*" so often, that I was afraid you would think that was your name. And you did the funniest things. Even when you toddled into the middle of Mom's Tupperware party all naked and squatted down and left a little present in a stackable fridge-smart burp-n-seal casserole dish, we all just laughed. And when you overhead everyone talking about Hurricane Katrina and thought you had done something wrong, I ran to hold you and take care of you. Katrina, you were such a sweet little girl, all that I can say is…

What happened to you?

Victory

They said we were too short. And then they told us we were too young. And when we said we wanted to try anyway, they laughed at us.

Only one team from our district would get to go to the basketball quarter finals, and we were the youngest and smallest to try out. All the other teams just saw the quarter finals as a stopping-off place. They wanted to go all the way to the championship. But we would have been happy to be picked for anything. We just wanted to stop them from laughing.

So we gave it our best. I'd like to say this story ends with my team winning the quarter finals. But I can't. I can't say that because we won the quarters and went on to the semifinals. And then the finals. And when our little team won the basketball championship, no one was laughing. Well, no one but us.

Pizza Face

Mallory stood up from the lunchroom table, eyeing the hot guys who had just seated themselves next to us. I probably should have told her that the zipper on her tight jeans had broken open, and I could see that it was Thursday because she was wearing her pink and white Thursday undies. We strutted past the boys, and as expected, they fell apart with laughter. Out in the hall, I told her I'd seen the broken zipper, but couldn't resist letting her strut. "Oh," she purred, "if you'd only told me, I could have let you know why the boys were really laughing." She pointed to my reflection in the trophy case. Yep, it was Thursday all right 'cause Thursday is pizza day in the cafeteria, and I had a big ole slice of somebody's leftover three-cheese on my behind.

All the Marbles

I used to think of myself as quite a clown. One of my tricks was to put straws and marbles and tinker toys into my mouth, ears, and nose. It sure made my siblings laugh. And one night, I got really tickled too, inhaled, and sucked a marble up my nose. I started to freak out. My brother suggested sticking the garden hose in my mouth and holding the other nostril shut. A second brother was describing a technique that involved firecrackers when my hysterical screams brought my dad. A few calming words and a little cooking oil, and I was saved. But let me tell you that I'm much more careful now about where I lose my marbles.

Insanity Plea

While trying to break into showbiz, I am keeping my job at the nursing home. One of my patients there is forever asking me to find her invisible friend "Gypsy." Another one is certain she is dating my father.

I used to laugh at the fragile eighty-six-year-old who entertained me with bizarre stories of her life of crime. Looking up her history, I found that she just finished serving her tenth jail sentence.

Another patient is convinced that we are trying to poison her with milk of magnesia. Her point is that, even if you could catch a magnesia, how could you milk it?

My coworkers say, with a secure career as a nurse, why would I want to be around all those crazy showbiz people. I just smile and answer, "Continuing education."

Peed Off

Do you have to pee every time I say hello? I mean, I bet I said hi thirty times today, and no one—*no one*—smiled at me and then peed on the floor. I know it's your way of saying you love me, but couldn't you just wag your tail or jump up and slobber on me or even hump my leg? I used to think it was because you needed to go out and potty, but even after you've watered every bush in the neighborhood, all I have to do is step out for one second, and I come back in to April showers. What, do you keep a reserve hidden somewhere? Do you have a backup tank like the Winnebago? I don't mean to scare you, but I have been thinking about taking drastic measures. Yes, either you get some bladder control, or I'm afraid I'm going to have to resort to...*doggy diapers.*

Sour Note

As I stand before you all, I have only one thought: my mom can't make me shut up now. So here goes.

I love you, Mom, but you are old. Stop trying to act cool when my friends are around. I mean, culottes are so ninety years ago.

Please don't sing anymore. You are not Taylor Swift, you are not Rihanna, and even Beyonce isn't Beyonce anymore, so please have mercy and just hum. Quietly.

And finally, please stop trying to join in when I'm dancing with my friends. I know the Charleston was a big hit when you were a child, and you probably loved to waltz back during the Civil War, but times have changed.

Please let me enjoy being young. You just be a mom. Be old. You've earned it.

Dumpster Diving

I can't believe my own parents are making me go Dumpster diving!

What if someone sees me?

What if the Department of Child Abuse comes along and takes me away from you? Then you'll be sorry!

I know you told me not to take my retainer out in restaurants, but how was I to know we'd get a waiter who cleaned our table every two seconds?

This is so humiliating. And slimy. And stinky!

And that homeless man is staring holes through me.

Oh, wait, I think I found—no—wait a second...

Mom. Dad. Something's...*moving.*

Nature's Miracle

I learned a lot about life on a recent tour of South Africa. Off to the side of the road, I saw a water buffalo in distress. After watching for a moment, I realized she was giving birth! Now, I'm a city girl, so this was a big deal for me. I kept my distance, not wanting to disturb her or put myself in danger, but I clicked away with my digital camera. It was fascinating! The entire thing only took minutes, but was both agonizing and beautiful to watch. Afterwards, this huge beast actually seemed...well, *proud.*

When I returned home, I shared these beautiful shots with my church group. It was an amazing experience, but never more so than when our pastor pointed out that the buffalo had only deposited a huge mound of poop.

Spandex Workout

(All done while doing very distinctive '80s dance moves) Oh yeah, I belong to a gym. It keeps me fit. Keeps me looking young too. These twenty-one-year-olds got nuthin' on me! I catch a glimpse of myself in the mirror sometimes, and I think...I look gooooood. And with this iPod stuck in my ear, nobody knows I'm sweatin' to the oldies. *(Touching the earpiece) Sheena Easton, you go, baby!* And since I got rid of my leg warmers and headbands, these kids just think I'm one of them. *(With lots of cheerleader movements) Oh, Mickey, you're so fine, you're so fine, you blow my mind—beep, beep! (Looking off to the side)* Hey, what are you laughin at? Jane Fonda what? Oh, I'm gonna have to get all Jack Lalane on you now. *(Takes off after them.)*

Role Model

(Raising hand)   Excuse me, Professor.

I sat in your economics class all semester and listened carefully. You've brought some sanity to the insanity of money and budgets and balances.

Yesterday, I stood in line at the ATM. People's Bank on Church Street—ring a bell? Apparently, the ATM took your money and refused to give you a receipt. You jumped and threatened and screamed. If I'm not mistaken, I think you even put a gypsy curse on the machine.

No, I'm not telling this to make fun or put you in a bad light. I wanted you to know how great that made me feel. If *you* can have a hissy fit at the bank, I guess the rest of us aren't so crazy after all.

Standard Gear

It's not weird; it's perfectly normal! Putting your panty hose under my clothes before I go hunting helps keep me warm! It creates a buffer zone. It holds the heat next to your body. It keeps the cold pants away from my legs—it's a scientific fact!

C'mon, baby, all the other guys are doing it.

Look, this doesn't have to be weird. I promise you won't even know I'm wearing them. All you'll see is your big old macho huggy bear ready to go out and slaughter some helpless little animals.

Yeah, that's all better now, huh? So let me go get dressed before the other guys get here, okay?

Um, baby, you wouldn't happen to have a pair of black fishnets would you?

Best Man

My best friend was marrying the nicest guy in the world. She was radiant; he was gorgeous. I told him over and over, "Teddy, you are so perfect for her." "Teddy, you are so wonderful." "Teddy, I'm so glad you guys found each other."

I had been asked to toast the bride and groom. As I spoke, everyone looked embarrassed. Was my dress torn? Had I slipped out of my low-cut bridesmaid dress? Never mind. I ended with a hearty, "Here's to Teddy and Renee, the perfect couple!"

And on my way back to my seat, I remembered, all by myself, that Teddy was her ex, and she had just married Frank.

Sack Lunch

This isn't my lunch. What do I do now? All the brown bags looked the same; I thought I recognized the grease stains, but I guess all grease stains look alike too. Okay, no bags left, so someone has mine. And...everyone's happily munching, so I guess I should just shut up and eat this one. No going back now. I'll just eat this one. What is that smell? Oh, no. This is either a very old meatloaf or some kind of furry cheese. *(Cutting eyes to the side)* Oh, please don't look at me like that; it's not me—it's the meat. Or cheese. *(Peering at something.)* With...ants. There are ants on this. And they are dead. Probably suicide. Yep, the smell got 'em.

Dinner Music

I like to eat at *Cracker Barrel* because they have a store and really good food and you don't have to listen to the waiters run around singing *Happy Birthday*. But one night, we just started to dig into our food when a waitress with big red hair stood up in front of the fireplace and yelled, "Hey, everybody, it's Patsy's birthday, and we're gonna *sing!*" She had a big voice that sounded like she smoked lots of cigarettes. She sang loud and scratchy, and most everybody kept on eating and didn't sing with her. How embarrassing! Afterwards, I told my mom she must be new. My mom said, "No, she was probably just from New Jersey."

Girls' Bikes

When I was little, I took out my sister's bike for a joyride. She'd warned me never to do that because girls' bikes were different. Hey, I knew that! Any bozo could see that they didn't have the bar like a boy's bike. So I jumped on her bike and started down the hill toward the neighbor's house. I sped faster and faster—it was fantastic! As I neared their house, I applied the brakes. Nothing. I pumped the pedals like crazy. Nothing! No brakes at all! Well, in the end, my parents found out what I'd done. They found out because the neighbors called to tell them that I was sitting on their couch with them, and I had entered through their picture window. I found out it's not just the bar that's different on a girl's bike. The brakes are on the *handles*.

Last Date

I'm letting you go. I'm walking away. It's over. It's not your fault. You just hold too many memories for me, and now they tear at my heart.

It's not you. It's me. I've changed. I used to love seeing you. You made me feel safe. You made me happy. I used to love coming home to you. But now, I look at you, and you just seem so empty.

And don't think this is easy for me. After I leave, I'm going to miss you. And wonder what's going on with you. Is there someone new? Are you being taken care of? I know I'll be tempted to drive by, just to catch a glimpse. But I won't. Seeing you with someone else would hurt more than not seeing you at all.

So it's over. I'm walking away now. I'm turning out your lights.

They'll be putting up the For Sale sign tomorrow.

Big Impression

I am not a sports fan, but my new boyfriend was, and I so wanted to impress him. On one of our first dates, he took me to a Braves game. I faked my way through and learned a few things as the game went along. Did you know there's a ball player named Chipper? How cute! So this Chipper Jones guy was holding the bat, and this other guy threw a ball at him, and he swung at it and hit it and—wow! It went sailing high, and all the other players were running after it! Well, the crowd was cheering as Chipper ran around the bases and headed for home. I was so excited! The crowd screamed, and I leapt to my feet and yelled, "Touchdown!" Suddenly, there was dead silence, followed by thousands of people laughing. Everyone in the stadium was laughing except for me. And my boyfriend. He just sat there. Staring at me. Up on the Jumbotron.

High Note

When I was in high school, I studied martial arts. During one match, my partner was well over six feet. Now, you may not believe it to look at me now, but in high school, I was pretty short. On this particular day, I was asked to demonstrate a kick to my opponent's face. So I crouch down, take a mighty leap, and extend my leg out as far as it will go. As I felt my leg make firm contact, I was so proud of myself. That is, until I looked at my partner's face, which was, at this point, just about even with mine. It seems that I made contact, all right. But with the height difference, the point of contact was not his face, but...um...somewhat lower. The up side of this story is that my former opponent now has a successful career as a tenor.

Direct Approach

I'm a pediatrician, and although the young ones are my patients, I also need to communicate clearly with the parents. One day, while attempting to do just that, the adorable little one kept interrupting. "You're short," she said.

"Well, yes I am," I replied, and resumed my talk with the mom.

"Why are you so short?" she asked.

"Because this is how tall I am supposed to be," I answered.

"Are you going to grow?" she snapped.

"No, I don't think so."

"Why, why, why not?" she demanded. Of course, I kept my cool and remained patient with the little angel. But in my mind, I turned to her and said, "Because living on a steady diet of rude little girls cooked in castor oil has stunted my growth!"

Sometimes, it just sucks to be a grown-up.

Master Disaster Class

It wasn't my fault!

I guess I dozed off in lit class, but instead of just calling me from across the room, Ms. Deedles leaned right over me and screamed in my ear, "Wake up, Caroline!" and I jerked my head up and hit her in the nose with the back of my head. Then I fell over backwards and caught Wilbur's feet under my desk. He freaked out and tried to get up but fell over on top of Ms. Deedles whose nose was bleeding all over Muffy Carson, which made Muffy barf on Rhoda and Rhoda barfed on Harvey and Harvey tried to run out of the room, but passed out first from having a terrible phobia about blood and fell on the fire alarm, setting off the sprinklers. Which really did help by washing away some of the barf and blood.

It's all Ms. Deedles's fault! I believe she is evil and should be destroyed.

Bad Hair Day

Can you airbrush my hair once the headshots are done? I mean, can you Photoshop it out?

Believe it or not, I'm a normal person with normal hair. I haven't been recently electrocuted or badly frightened. It's just that my mom always wanted to be a hairstylist, but she never got the chance. Then when she found I was having headshots done…well, I couldn't stomp on her dream, could I?

And yes, I thought of brushing it out once I left the house, but the comb got stuck. It's still in there somewhere, along with bobby pins, a barrette, two scrunchies, some tissue paper, a can and a half of Aqua Net, and a portable hair dryer.

(Hissing, eyes wide in terror) Help me!

Buzz Cut

I used to snore really loud. I mean *Guinness Book of World Records* loud. This became such a problem that my dogs (who sleep with me) used to bury their heads under my cats (who also sleep with me). I snored so loud, in fact, that I had to have surgery. After the operation, we had a few quiet nights. Then the buzz saw noise woke my family again. My parents broke into my room, so upset that we were looking at more surgery. And there they found me sound asleep. And my dog...snoring. Just like me.

We took him to the vet, who told us my dog had learned the snoring from me.

"Why did he learn to snore like me?" I asked.

Then I heard my dad mutter, "Probably self-defense."

Snoot Full

Since you are my brother, I have to love you. I think that's required by law.

But I don't have to put up with your dog-poo, old-cheese, dirty-feet, monkey-butt smell.

I know Mom and Dad try to force you to clean up by locking you in the bathroom. But I don't think you ever turn on the water. I think you just sit in there and ferment. So I'll tell you what I'm going to do. I've collected an assortment of your old sneakers, T-shirts, and tighty-whities. I've kept them in a baggie out in the sun all week, along with some sulfur, garlic, and a raw egg. I shook a little used cat litter in there for seasoning. Now, if you do not take a complete, all-over, total submersion soapy bath every day from now on, I'm going to sneak into your room while you sleep, tie you down, and tape this bag over your face.

Be afraid. Be very afraid.

Long Night

It's been twelve hours now. Lord, if you'll just help me out of this, I'll never date again. We were just sitting on the coach talking when she said, "That sounds like my husband's car driving up. Get under the bed."

Husband?

I ask a girl out, it's usually, "Would you like to go out? What time should I pick you up? Where would you like to go?" I just never thought to add, "Oh, and are you running around on your maniac husband?"

Please, Lord, just let me out from under this bed. I never knew a man could sleep for twelve straight hours, or that any one person could make so many bodily noises during those twelve hours. I'm scared. I'm tired. I'm hungry.

Oooh. A Tic Tac.

Cleaning House

Do you know *why* I'm a clean-freak? Because I grew up with *you* as a sister!

You're like that kid Pig-Pen in the cartoon—you walk around in a permanent cloud of dirt. I have to follow you with the Dirt Devil, just so I can get through the house. You could never get lost—we'd just follow the trail of burrito wrappers and apple cores that you leave behind you. When you get up off my sofa, you leave a silhouette—my living room looks like a crime scene with chalk corpse outlines all over the place! And you have to be the only female on the planet who manages to *miss* the toilet seat! How do you do that—by standing up? Do you know that when you visit, my cat sleeps in her litter box because it's the cleanest spot in the house?

You're a biohazard. You're a landfill. You're a toxic waste dump. You're the three-mile island of sisters!

Don't set that down there! Use a coaster.

Chinatown

Remember Chinatown? One moment we were looking through shop windows and neon lights, and then...where were we? When did it get so dim and empty? One second, there was music, and then, in a blink, nothing but the echo of our footsteps on grimy pavement. I realized then what grown-ups meant when they talked about feeling your heart sink because that's just how I felt. My stomach turned over, and I couldn't find the air. Then I felt your hand. Heavens, you must have been even more frightened than I, but I didn't feel it. Your hand was warm and your voice steady as you pointed out our shadows on the alley walls and how they grew and shrank, rose and fell, but always stayed together as we walked. My eyes were filled with the play of dark and light and my ears with the sound of your voice. There was no room for fear; no place for it to enter.

Made in United States
North Haven, CT
07 September 2024